# LIMBERLOST

'As close to flawless as any book I have read in years.'
Jessie Greengrass

'Confirms Robbie Arnott as a masterly writer.'
*The Times*

'Arnott is at the peak of his game.'
Barry Reynolds, *Herald Sun*

'Stunning…Not a word is wasted…Powerful, lyrical.'
Claire Nichols, ABC Arts

'Luminously told…Genuinely transcendent.'
Melissa Harrison, *Guardian* (UK)

'Lyrical language…Powerfully real characters.'
*Sydney Morning Herald*

'Beautiful…A magnificent piece of work.'
Jonathan Green, ABC RN *Bookshelf*

'A striking book, with lingering resonance.'
Fiona Wright, *Saturday Paper*

'Magnificent…A must-read novel.'
*Good Reading*

'Filled with wonder…Transcendent and immersive.'
Zachary Prior, *Big Issue*

'Extraordinarily imaginative…His writing is so exquisite.'
ABC TV *Weekend Breakfast*

Praise for
# THE RAIN HERON

'Genuinely and completely magnificent.'
Robert Lukins

'Sharp and original...A beautiful novel.'
Laura Elvery

'Singlehandedly reinventing Australian literature.'
Bram Presser

'Fantastic...Diamond-sharp prose.'
Kawai Strong Washburn

'A timeless and poignant meditation.'
*Guardian*

'Mesmerising and beautifully written.'
*Scotsman*

'One of Australia's leading young novelists.'
*Canberra Times*

'Arnott's sentences are truly a pleasure to read.'
*Saturday Paper*

'Literary art...An original, compelling work.'
*Australian*

'A gorgeous and spellbinding eco-fantasy.'
*Buzzfeed*

'Dazzlingly visual...Beautifully rendered.'
*Los Angeles Review of Books*

Praise for
# FLAMES

'A strange and joyous marvel.'
Richard Flanagan

'A stunning new Australian voice.'
Rohan Wilson

'Visionary...A brilliant and wholly original debut.'
Gail Jones

'A vivid and bold new voice.'
Danielle Wood

'Delightful...Enchanting.'
*Guardian*

'Startlingly good...Stylistically adventurous, gorgeous.'
*Australian*

'Unique and memorable.'
*Kill Your Darlings*

'Exuberantly creative...Strange and occasionally brutal.'
*Australian Book Review*

'Breathtaking...A poetically wild and wicked imagination.'
*SA Weekend*

'Gloriously audacious...It bowled me sideways.'
*New Zealand Herald*

'Assured, funny and highly imaginative.'
*Stuff NZ*

Robbie Arnott's acclaimed debut, *Flames* (2018), won a *Sydney Morning Herald* Best Young Novelist award and a Tasmanian Premier's Literary Prize, and was shortlisted for a Victorian Premier's Literary Award, a New South Wales Premier's Literary Award, a Queensland Literary Award, the Readings Prize for New Australian Fiction and the Not the Booker Prize. His follow-up, *The Rain Heron* (2020), won the *Age* Book of the Year award, and was shortlisted for the Miles Franklin Literary Award, the ALS Gold Medal, the Voss Literary Prize, an Adelaide Festival Award and the William Saroyan International Prize for Writing. He lives in Hobart.

@RobbieArnott

# LIMBERLOST
## ROBBIE ARNOTT

TEXT PUBLISHING MELBOURNE AUSTRALIA

The Text Publishing Company acknowledges the Traditional Owners of the country on which we work, the Wurundjeri people of the Kulin Nation, and pays respect to their Elders past and present.

textpublishing.com.au

The Text Publishing Company
Wurundjeri Country, Level 6, Royal Bank Chambers, 287 Collins Street, Melbourne Victoria 3000 Australia

Published by The Text Publishing Company, 2022
Reprinted 2022 (three times)

Cover art and design by W. H. Chong
Page design by Rachel Aitken
Typeset by J&M Typesetting

Printed and bound in Australia by Griffin Press, an Accredited ISO AS/ NZS 14001:2004 Environmental Management System printer

ISBN: 9781922458766 (paperback)
ISBN: 9781922791047 (ebook)

A catalogue record for this book is available from the National Library of Australia.

**C⦿PYRIGHT**AGENCY
CULTURAL FUND

*This project was supported by the Copyright Agency's Cultural Fund. Parts of the manuscript were completed while Robbie Arnott was the 2021 University of Tasmania Hedberg Writer-in-Residence.*

*For my family*

In the economy of Nature nothing is ever lost.

—*Gene Stratton-Porter*

# 1

IT WAS BELIEVED a whale had gone mad at the mouth of the river. Several fishing boats had been destroyed in acts of violence so extraordinary they were deemed inhuman. Each attack had come at dusk, while the boats were passing the heads on their way back to port—the same area where plumes of spray were supposedly erupting from the water. Transport ships reported powerful, mournful vibrations ringing through their hulls. Gulls flew strangely; cormorants seemed skittish. Ocean swimmers' strokes were thrown out of rhythm by a high, ancient melody that rose through the brine. A fluked tail had been seen troubling the waves.

Ned was five when all this happened. In later years he struggled to remember the incidents clearly, but at the time it was all anyone was talking about. The animal had been harpooned far down south, someone's uncle said, and after fleeing north was now visiting vengeance on any ship it encountered. Another version of that story claimed the harpoon had lodged in the whale's brain, turning it feral and vicious. Another was that the whalers had missed the beast but not its pod, and the creature had been driven insane after witnessing the slaughter of its family.

There were other theories too, ones that didn't include whaling, ideas of lunar imbalances and divine judgement, although they weren't paid much attention. Most held the southern whalers responsible for fouling the animal's mind. There was talk of writing letters, demanding reparations, getting the council involved.

'It's nonsense,' Ned's father told his children. He'd caught them whispering about the wrecks at the dinner table, unaware he'd returned from the orchard.

'There is no whale,' he said. 'No monster. Fishermen do three things: they drink too much, and they make things up.'

He took off his coat and hung it on a hook by the door.

'What's the third thing,' asked Ned's eldest brother, Bill.

Their father levered himself into his chair. 'Occasionally they catch fish.'

But their father's words did not convince them; the story of the mad whale had sunk too deep into their minds. Ned's sister, Maggie, was old enough to restrain herself from contributing to the gossip, but Bill and Toby, their middle brother, talked about it constantly.

Ned heard everything, and their conversations filled him with obsessive dread. All day he thought of the smashed ketches and skiffs, of an unseen giant with a blade snagged in its brain. At night his dreams were flooded with blood-foamed water. For a week he woke sweating and screaming until, when his exhausted father demanded to know the cause of his turmoil, he revealed that his nightmares were of the murderous, hell-sent whale.

'Right,' his father said the next morning, toast cooling on his plate. 'We're going to the river mouth tonight. I'll show you the truth of this so-called man killer.'

Late that afternoon he took his sons to a nearby jetty, where they piled into a small boat their father had borrowed from a neighbour, one of the only boats in the area with a motor. Their father fiddled with the greasy machine, and his solemn care gave Ned and his brothers the sense that a large favour had been called in. But none of them said anything. They were all thinking of the whale.

Soon their father got the engine working, got it growling, and for the next hour they motored along the river until the course of the water straightened and the sea beyond it widened to fill the dusk. When they reached the mouth, all that remained of the sun was a half-disc of orange light over the western hills. Their father killed the motor.

They stayed there, bobbing on the light swell. The last sliver of sun vanished and the sky darkened into a clear night. Their father leaned back in the boat, appearing to contemplate the thick pattern of starlight above them. The wind was cold. Ned and his brothers shivered into their collars as they waited for the whale to explode out of the river and paste them into the waves.

# 2

A DECADE LATER Ned lay on a wet bank watching a rabbit graze. It was dawn. The early light spread through the fibres of the animal's fur. Ned aimed his rifle, took the shot, missed. The gun's crack threw his prey into a sprint, and it blurred into the bracken gathered beneath a stand of nearby blue gums. Beyond the trees the land fell away, lowering to meet the river, whose wide teal face was here and there dragged apart by deep and changeable eddies.

Ned had wasted a bullet, and the sound of his shot would have sent any other rabbits into hiding. He stared at the distant water, wrestling his frustration, feeling that he had ruined the morning. His mood eased on his way back to the house, when he checked a trap he'd placed in a run beneath one of the fences.

When he'd set the trap the previous evening, he'd worried that its trigger was too light, that any passing creature would set it off before entering the radius of its jaws. But a fat rabbit lay in the dirt of the run, metal teeth sunk into its neck. Except for the puncture wounds, its coat was unmarred. Ned removed the animal, then reset the trap. He ran his fingers over his kill, noting the thickness of the fur, the rigidity of death. Felt bright heat in his throat.

He resumed walking through Limberlost, his father's orchard, the rabbit swinging stiff in his hand. Smoke hazed from the house's chimney. Apple trees in a nearby paddock had taken on the glow of dawn. At Ned's back the river shone, teal blinking into slate and cerulean, revealing a greater truth of colour.

~

It was summer, and in the long blond light of the season Ned aimed to kill as many rabbits as he could. Their pelts could be sold to the army, who made them into slouch hats for soldiers. He had no other way of making money. In previous summers his father might have paid him for helping out on the orchard, but with the war on that was no longer possible.

If he killed enough rabbits he might earn enough to buy his own boat—something he'd imagined ever since his father had taken Ned and his brothers to meet the mad whale on that clear, star-rich night. Nothing fancy, just a small, single-sailed dinghy he could run into the river. Out on the water he could sail wherever he liked, from downstream where the current ran fresh to the broad estuary in the north. Squid-filled reefs, forested coves, schools of flashing salmon, trenches of snapper, lonely jetties, private beaches on whose cold sands he could burn hidden fires—all would be open to him if he had a boat. If he killed enough rabbits.

It was already January. Fewer than ten had found his

traps or caught his bullets—barely enough to buy an oar, Ned suspected. Yet already his thoughts were wet and salty, his mind roughened by windburn. Always he thought of the boat: how he'd care for it, where he'd pilot it, what he'd feel in the grip of its planks, against the whip of the wind. Most of all he wondered what his brothers would say when they returned from the war and saw him out there on the water, riding the rips, guiding the rudder with a practised palm, not looking back to acknowledge their presence on the shore until he felt ready.

~

As he neared the house Ned saw his father on the porch, a mug of tea in his hand. Steam lifted from the cup. He was looking out at the trees, but as Ned approached his gaze shifted to his son's hand. He saw the carcass. Sipped at the steam.

'You'd be happy with that.'

Ned nodded, held the rabbit out for inspection.

His father took the corpse and stretched it by its rear legs and ears, pulling it taut. He studied the fur, the wounds. Subdued approval showed on his face.

Ned felt pride heat his cheeks. Impressing his father couldn't compare with impressing Bill, or even Toby—the old man was too strange, too distant in his quiet moods and shifting habits—but the approval was still important.

As the rabbit turned in his father's hands, Ned thought of what he'd do next: how he would slide a knife into its belly fur and untether the skin from the flesh. He'd drape the pelt over a wire hanger in the empty apple shed—every piece of fruit his father had grown last season had been requisitioned by the army and taken to the new cannery in Beaconsfield—where it would dry, alongside the others he planned on collecting that week. He thought of how he'd harvest these other pelts, his mind roaming across the orchard, remembering paths that resembled the one where he'd set his successful trap. He pictured the bracken that the rabbit he'd missed had run into, thought of ways to position himself closer to the scrub. He imagined himself breathing slowly, squeezing the rifle's trigger with an ease that approached boredom. He saw more traps springing, more iron fangs. His dreams inched to their inevitable conclusion: the boat. The lap of dark waves against the hull, the hoisting of a stiff sail...

'It'll make a fine hat.'

His father's voice cut through Ned's visions. The old man was looking down at him, a new crease in his face. His fingers were deep in the rabbit's fur, combing back and forth.

Ned cooled. 'I hope so.'

Unease sank through him. He hadn't told anyone why he was hunting rabbits—not his friends, not his father. When he eventually brought the boat home, he imagined the occasion would be a double surprise: his acquisition of such a thing, and that he'd kept his mission secret. He'd have his boat, and he'd have people's shock at the casual totality of his competence. Two victories.

But with his father closely inspecting his kill, he realised he hadn't accounted for how the old man would perceive Ned's hunting. Now he saw it: how his father's oldest boys had been pulled to a distant leviathan of a war, beyond scope or compre-hension. This very morning—as every morning, wherever they were—their faces were hardening into rough shapes beneath the shade of rabbit-pelt hats. Such smart hats, both stiff and soft, so similar to the one their father had worn in his own war, a quarter-century earlier, on his own foreign battlefields—high-cliffed coves, grey worlds of ice-mud—a hat that had darkened his eyes as he was torn apart and recast into this quiet, strange man who remained out of reach and unknowable to his own sons.

And all the while his youngest remained at home, spending his free months selflessly avoiding leisure in order to provide rabbit pelts to the army for the production of slouch hats. Ned saw how it looked, how he had misrepresented his intentions. How he'd drawn a nobler image of himself in his father's eyes than could ever be true. The tea steam snagged in his nose, bitter in the dew.

His father's hands were still running over the corpse. He was no longer looking at Ned, or at the orchard, or at anything in particular.

Ned felt a quickening in his blood. His eyes itched. With slow, unspoken statements, he began convincing himself that his father had not been deceived. That he really was going hunting for the sole purpose of producing those proud, necessary slouch hats. That while his brothers were at war, he was playing the only part he could. The pelts were for hats; the boat was incidental.

~

After breakfast he went to work in the orchard with his father, and the two or so hours he spent among the trees, working with his eyes and hands—checking fruit, looking for blight—slowly reordered his mind. Things became clearer. He was spending his summer hours hunting, and his father approved: that was all that was happening. It did not require overthinking.

That afternoon he went fishing with his neighbour. Jackbird was short for fifteen, even shorter than Ned, with a habit of fidgeting. They'd been neighbours their whole lives, and outside summer they shared a class at school. Ned had once dragged Jackbird from a rip current and squeezed the ocean out of his skinny chest. A year later Jackbird had pelted a rock into the cheek of an older boy who'd thrown Ned to the ground in the schoolyard. Dashed a wet hole in the flesh that whistled whenever the boy breathed, until it healed a couple of weeks later.

They fished from a jetty that pushed out into the river. Ned held a finger on his line, feeling for the tremor of a bite that did not come. Perhaps the day was too clear, the sun too bright. Bill had once said fish didn't feed in good weather, and Bill was the best fisherman he knew. It was something to do with wind stirring them into action, or rain flooding oxygen into the salt-water, or that direct sunlight made them sluggish. Ned tried to remember, but he'd only ever overheard Bill saying these things to Maggie, or maybe Toby.

Jackbird flicked a thumb against his line. 'Any bites?'

'Not a nibble.'

Jackbird kept fiddling with his rod, lifting and dropping his sinker, trailing it across the bottom. He checked his bait. It hung firm on the hook.

'Be better with a boat.'

Ned flinched. 'Where would we get a boat?'

'Just saying. Better with a boat.'

'Course it'd be better with a boat. But we don't have a boat. And unless you know something I don't, that isn't going to change.' His voice was flat, even as his blood thumped.

They were quiet for a while after that. Ned hadn't wanted to think of boats. He remembered his father's fingers, roaming through the fur. His brothers. He was angry that Jackbird had mentioned it, wished his friend would be content with what they had, with this sunny, windless day.

Jackbird reeled his line in again. 'You heard from Toby?'

'Not for a while. He should still be in the reserve force. They're only meant to be sent in if things get worse.'

'Uh-huh.' Jackbird cast out, let his sinker drop. 'Reckon we'll get called up?'

'Papers say it's winding down.'

'True.' He raised his rod to his shoulder. Held it like a rifle, aiming at a cluster of yachts that were tethered to buoys just off the shore. 'What about Bill?'

Ned was watching Jackbird's line tangle. 'What about him?'

'Anything in the paper about his division?'

'Not since Singapore fell.'

'Any letters?'

'Not that I know of.'

Jackbird jerked his rod, swung his feet.

Ned saw the hesitation in him. 'If you're going to say something, say it.'

Still Jackbird hesitated. But he couldn't stop the question coming out. 'Your old man all right out there on the orchard?'

The thump returned to Ned's pulse. 'You want the Christmas letter in January? You want the family teacake recipe?'

'All right, all right. Just asking. People talk.'

'That they do.'

Again they went quiet. The sun lowered and its light began filtering through the trees, shadowing the water. Jackbird got a few nibbles, or convinced himself he did, but didn't bring anything to the surface. After a while he began talking about how a hawk had been taking their chickens, and how his little sister, Callie, had taken to parading through the paddocks with their father's shotgun, determined to scare it off or even blast it from the sky.

Ned tried to picture Callie with the iron heft of a shotgun in her arms. She couldn't have been older than thirteen. Straw-haired, straight-faced. Hard as a walnut. The shotgun almost made sense.

The whole time they were at the jetty, Ned felt nothing trouble his hook. He told himself that he did not mind—this summer he had cast himself as a rabbit hunter. A lack of fish did not matter. But still he felt sour. Twice now he'd spoken sharply to Jackbird. And there was the matter of the slouch hats, of his father's misplaced pride, of his brothers' faraway war-shadows. And that he really did want a boat: wanted it more than he'd ever wanted anything. The thirst for it was thick in him, and no amount of shame or resolve could shake it from his veins.

So as the river darkened, as the fish remained untempted, Ned's boat dreams returned to where they had begun: the evening of the mad whale. The memory gave the rest of his afternoon—which was otherwise biteless and golden—a deep pull of terror, of strangeness and starlight.

# 3

TEN YEARS LATER, Ned again thought of the evening of
the mad whale. By then he'd left Limberlost for the forests of
the east. He was working in a logging crew to fell a large copse
of manna gums—ancient hardwoods ghostly in colour and
immense in height, some rising a hundred yards into the air to
flail their leaves against the sky's cheek. Aromatic, bloodlike sap
ran from the wounds the men hacked into their trunks.

Ned was the youngest in the crew. He was also the foreman.
He'd got the job because he didn't drink much, and the other
loggers drank like they were being paid to. At the end of each
day they returned to their bush camp, where the foresters
mirrored the violence they'd wreaked on the White Knights—
the name they'd given to the pale, towering mannas—in the
way they treated their own bodies. They poured lakes of beer
down their throats, as well as rivers of brownish, burning rum.
Spread out in the shadows of the White Knights, they sang and
fought and screamed until they vomited, cried for their wives

and crashed into their swags.

When they'd put him in charge, Ned's superiors had given him a simple mission: stay sober enough to make sure chaos didn't overwhelm the camp. During the working day he was nominally in charge of operations, but the loggers were experienced men, leathered by decades of warring with the trees. They rarely felt the need to speak to each other, not even when they felled the largest of the Knights, lopped off the limbs and hauled the pale-glowing trunks onto their flatbed truck. None of this required Ned's oversight, although the loggers usually remembered to squint at the dropping sun and wait for his nod before knocking off for the day.

Ned drove the truck back to camp as the men began drinking in the back. Through the night he'd smile and recline and sip at a single bottle of lager as the men twisted themselves into goblins of the forest, drunk as much on the sweet-sticky sap that leaked from their vanquished foes as the liquor they gulped. Ned woke them at dawn, rolled them into the truck, drove back to the latest patch of mutilated forest and poured them onto their cold axes, their sap-bloody saws.

One night, after a particularly arduous day battling the Knights, the talk at camp turned lewd. There was talk of whores, of cunts, of buggery. It was intimated that splinters suffered in fucking a waxed tree hollow were ultimately preferable to the long-term wounds inflicted by a marriage. Ned did not consider himself prudish, but he did not feel comfortable listening to this talk, especially while sober. After throwing a log on the fire he walked back to his seat, then kept walking into the night, unnoticed by the hollering loggers.

He moved slowly through the trees. With each careful step he could hear less of the raucous conversation. Voices faded to barks and yips. Starlight filtered down, revealing lumpen shapes, wet foliage. Soon he reached a swollen creek, and its heavy trickling washed away the remaining racket of the camp.

Ned sat, hoping the night chill and forest quiet would cool his thoughts. But soon he was disturbed. A harsh growl rang through the bush, a call of animal fury. More followed— deeper, guttural snarls, as well as high-ringing yowls of despair, sounds of fleshy terror. In the cacophony Ned could discern rage, indignation, pain and, most prominently, an anguished message of insatiable hunger. These night-screams bled into his ears. He could no longer hear the water.

He knew what these noises were. The devils had made a kill—or, more likely, stolen one from a quoll—and were fighting over the flesh. He'd heard screams like these many times, and was familiar with the horror the ravenous beasts inflicted upon each other as they fed. But every other time he'd heard devils in the night he'd had company—his father, his brothers, Jackbird. Never before had he sat in cold darkness, far from home, and listened to the bush's orchestra of terror in such detail.

It was this moment, as he felt again the liquid dread of unseen monsters, that brought him back to the night of the mad whale. The sensation was so similar to that boat trip, brought about by similar circumstances: an evening of demons, the potential for carnage. He shivered, realising he was cold. The forest's chill had never been a problem by the fire with the other men, but here by the stream it had stripped all the heat off his skin.

He'd shivered at the river mouth too. The wind had been harsh, ocean-cold, and he recalled how at one point he'd curled himself into the folds of a thick woollen jacket. It hadn't been his, he was sure of that—he hadn't owned a coat until he was a teenager. And it hadn't been his father's—that would have been far too large. It must have belonged to Toby or Bill. Ned couldn't recollect which of them had given it to him. It made sense, for a variety of reasons, for it to have been Toby, although he was just as likely to have teased Ned for showing weakness.

But Toby had been sitting on the other side of the boat to Ned, with their father between them. Ned had huddled next to Bill as they waited for the whale's judgement. Surely Bill hadn't lent Ned his coat? Ned could barely remember his eldest brother ever talking to him. Yet he remembered the warmth of the wool.

# 4

IN THE WEEK that followed his fruitless fishing trip with Jackbird, Ned killed fourteen rabbits—by far his biggest haul of the season. He hadn't done anything all that different, although he'd started getting up earlier, often before sunrise, waiting in the darkness until the world warmed and the rabbits twitched out into the open. He learned to let his pulse settle before squeezing the trigger, instead of rushing to fire as soon as they revealed themselves. As his accuracy improved he began to know the shape each rabbit would make in death, just from how they sat on the grass. In the moment before he fired, he saw a premonition of the form the rabbit would fling into when its flesh caught his bullet—snapping and collapsing into stillness.

His traps were more successful too. He'd learned to distinguish between earth that was bare due to a lack of moisture and soil that had been scraped by a rabbit squirming under a fence. He began targeting these under-fence trails, setting traps in the centre of the dirt and concealing them with scatterings of dry grass. Only a few yielded rabbits, but the ones that didn't were usually triggered. Ned scored these near-catches as ties, and reset each trap with minor variations.

He enjoyed the game of trapping, of finding the runs and outsmarting the animals. But he did not like treading through purple dawns to find rabbits still living in his traps, their legs rent, blood matting their fur, primitive terror vibrating off their whiskers. Usually they were dead, even if the jaws hadn't closed around their necks or heads; usually the trauma of the trapping would halt the thump of their hearts. But on those mornings where he found them alive, Ned felt a yellow-green surge in his stomach, and couldn't rush to kill them quickly enough. They were feral, he reminded himself, as he held their ruined bodies firm and placed a boot over their necks. They were pests. The only true use they had was to serve in death as slouch hats. And yet he felt a huge relief when they ceased shivering under his foot. In these moments he would look away from the rabbit to the sky, the glowing trees, the wakening river, as if the tranquillity of the orchard could remove him from what he'd done.

Each morning after breakfast he'd skin the rabbits on an old grey stump. With practice he'd reduced the mistakes he made with each pelt, as well as the time it took to remove them. First he'd take his knife to the hock joints, cutting through the tendons, before twisting off the paws. Then he'd make a small slice into the belly fur, making sure his blade did not slip into the flesh. From here he wriggled his fingers into the aperture and began working the skin from the muscle, freeing the stomach, sliding off the back, reversing both sets of legs through the holes where he'd removed the feet.

He did this carefully, meticulously, at all times remaining conscious of the shape and quality of the pelt. The only roughness came at the end of the process, when the final connection left between the fur and the flesh was at the neck. With a sharp yank he'd pull the pelt over the head, ripping it free. The carcass was left port-ruby and naked. The only hair remaining on the body was around its hacked hocks and on its now huge-seeming head.

Ned had learned skinning from Toby, who had learned it from Bill, who never revealed where he learned anything. While he was showing Ned where to make the incision in the belly, Toby had claimed that Bill could skin a rabbit without a knife.

'No idea how he does it,' Toby had said, a confused smile on his face. 'I tried figuring it out, but it happens so fast. Little twists, a pop, a rip, and the pelt's off. No blade in his hand.'

~

Towards the end of that bountiful week Ned removed a skin with such precision and artfulness that he felt the need to show his father, and to ask him something. It was mid-morning. He found his father in the orchard, standing before a juvenile apple tree. As Ned approached he stretched the pelt over his palms, showing his father the untorn skin, the bloodless fur. The neatness of the thing. But his father didn't appear to notice him. He gazed at the tree, eyes unfocused, until something caught his attention in the sky and he snapped his head up to stare at a cloud, his mouth moving, emitting no sounds.

Ned waited for a minute. When nothing changed he wandered back to his stump and knife.

Later in the day his father came to find him. He praised the skin he'd found hanging in the apple shed, along with the others Ned had harvested that week, and said that it would be a shame to let them spoil in the heat. He told Ned that he'd take him into town so he could sell them.

'I have some things to take care of as well. We'll go Tuesday.'

Ned nodded. He tried to remember the weather forecast for the days before Tuesday, tried to calculate how many skins he might add to his collection by then. His father turned to leave. As he began walking away Ned remembered what he'd wanted to ask the old man that morning.

'Toby said Bill could take a skin off without a knife.'

His father stopped. 'You don't want to do that. Not if you want to sell the fur. Looks flash, but it leaves the pelt raggedy, all torn up. Only good if you're in a hurry. If you need to feed the dogs before they rip into a lamb. You stick to the way you're doing it. You're doing it right.'

'But—'

'But what? What's all this butting—you meet a goat?'

'Sorry. But could he do it?'

His father turned to the orchard. Breathed at the trees. 'Who do you think taught him?'

~

The day before the trip to town, Ned's sister Maggie returned to Limberlost. She had been staying with a distant aunt in Hobart, training to be a teacher. The plan had been for her to spend the whole summer down south, taking extra courses, shortening the time it would take to gain her certificate. But circumstances had changed. Ned didn't know what circumstances, or how; he only learned from his father that Maggie was coming home the day before she arrived. And then there she was, marching down the gravel driveway, untroubled by the weight of her case.

By the time she'd eaten and washed, it was late. Ned was going to talk to her, but she seemed tired, and although she appeared pleased to see him, he read into her weariness that a conversation would only tire her further. After taking her case to her room he said goodnight.

As he lay in his bed he could hear her talking with his father, but he did not strain to make out the exchange. She was the eldest of the four siblings, the only one with a clear memory of their mother. It made sense for the two of them to talk, as they'd always done.

~

The next morning Ned found Maggie crouching by the chicken coop. He tried to figure out what she was doing, tried to think of something to say. He saw her fingers dip beneath the wire mesh, her face shifting with discovery.

Her hand stopped on a bare scratch of earth. Furrows were traced into the dirt, and the wire above was frayed and loose. She wedged her hand into the gap and, as she grimaced at the metal raking her skin, Ned must have moved or made an involuntary sound. Maggie glanced up. An expression passed over her face—a look somewhere between annoyance and humour. Ned raised a palm, words evading him.

Sometimes the love he felt for his sister flared so bright within him that he became uncommonly emotional—he'd feel an urge to show her his favourite knife, or to gabble at her without having anything to say. It had always been like this, even before she'd left for the capital, although he'd been too young to know her properly, and Maggie had been focused on school.

Now he felt it again. He also felt powerfully aware that he was the only brother she had left on the orchard. He had to make her laugh like Toby had, had to give her the quiet companionship Bill had somehow provided. He had to distract her from how far away they were. These swells of duty rose within him alongside his unpredictable pulses of love, and yet it was all he could do to stand before her, his palm raised, his mouth and mind a mess.

She withdrew her hand from the coop and stood up, brushing the dirt from her knees. 'Something's been at this,' she said.

'What was it?'

Maggie toed the scrape of dirt. 'I don't know. Cat, maybe. A devil.'

'Did it get in?'

'Not yet.'

She began walking around the rest of the enclosure. The chickens clucked at her from within the wire, venturing to peck at the gap she'd been investigating. Ned remembered what Jackbird had said about his sister and her shotgun.

'Could've been a hawk.'

Maggie looked up. 'A hawk.'

Ned avoided her eyes. 'A hawk's been after the chickens next door. Could be the same one.'

Maggie pointed at the scratched earth. 'You think a hawk landed here, grew paws and tried to dig its way in?'

'Well. No.'

'Hawks don't dig, oh great hunter. They swoop.'

She smiled, not cruelly, but still it twisted Ned's airways. He felt stupid and ashamed. He was going to argue, or he wasn't. He was going to push past her and see if he could demonstrate that the lines in the dirt could have just as easily been made by talons, or he was going to turn and walk away as fast as he could. He didn't know. And before he could do all of these things and none of them he heard his father calling, telling him to fetch his pelts, telling him it was time to go.

~

They were getting a ride into Beaconsfield with Jackbird's father. Ned's didn't have a truck of his own, and Jackbird's didn't mind doing favours like this.

They waited at the mouth of Limberlost's driveway, Ned with an armful of rabbit skins, his father with a ledger in his hands. Soon dust rose over a low rise, and Jackbird's father's off-white truck rolled into view. When it stopped beside them Ned's father got into the cab and Ned climbed into the tray. The truck lurched forward, and Ned braced himself as the orchards and river began receding. Rocks spat from the road into dry ditches.

In Beaconsfield they parked near the market. The men arranged to meet back at the truck an hour later, once they had finished their errands. Ned wasn't sure if his father was going to come with him to sell the skins, wasn't sure if he wanted him to. Jackbird's father strode away from them. Ned's glanced at his ledger, then at his son.

'Don't be late. Don't get cheated.'

He strode into the market. Ned felt a blink of coldness, before wriggling it off and making his way to Old Singline's shop.

Singline was a bastard about money but he was always buying. Ned had sold pelts to him the previous summer, when he'd begun hunting and trapping alone. He could sell directly to the army, but that would require travelling into Launceston, which was not possible without asking someone a favour that he knew was too great for his father to approve of. And while Singline—a man made mostly of lint, capillaries and brandy vapour—had haggled and pontificated until the afternoon turned stale, he had paid in cash. Ned figured him the easiest option, and perhaps his only one, although he was determined not to let that show in his negotiations.

He found the shop, straightened his pile of pelts, and pushed through the near-weightless door.

Afterwards, he wondered why he'd been nervous, why he'd felt the need to deepen his voice. Inside he'd found Singline a much-diminished figure. Perhaps he was ill; perhaps he was particularly hungover. Perhaps he had sons or nephews in uniform, or perhaps the war was wearing on him, the way it was with everyone. Ned didn't find out, didn't try to. He asked a fair price and, after an inspection and the briefest quibble about trap damage and pelt lustre, Singline agreed to it. Ned left the shop with a heavy pocket and a rush of feeling. Immediately he was doing calculations: how many could he kill, how much could he make.

Juggling these figures tempted him to walk past Beaconsfield's boatyard. Through the fence he'd be able to see the vast, airy field of watercraft. All dead in the dryness. The dinghies, the skiffs, the daggering hulls of the high-trailered yachts. Timber and paint and cloth and rope and iron and tin. In the half-hour he had spare Ned would be able to write them all into his memory; he'd be able to close his eyes and summon them for months, until summer cooled and fell.

Yet if his father finished his business early he might round the corner and see his son by the fence. Ned's ambitions would be plain. His father would read him in an instant, and the honourless greed that lay at the heart of Ned's hunting would be revealed.

That scenario was not something Ned could contemplate without starting to ache. So he criss-crossed the streets of Beaconsfield until it was time to meet at the truck, raising his eyes occasionally to the forested hills, to the tin roofs, the climbing spikes of the machinery that worked the nearby mine.

When he returned to the truck his father was already there. He looked at Ned with a question on his face. Ned hefted his pocket, showing the weight of the coins. His father lifted an eyebrow.

'You let him take you for a ride?'

'Asked a price. Got that price.'

The old man drew on a faint, tired smile. 'Well, you're either a hard lad or a thick one. Although you don't seem thick to me.'

Ned was strangled hot and mute by the compliment. In this moment life was not brimming with conflict, his skills not linked to guilt or shame.

His father leaned against a low stone wall, watching light

colour the hills. The ledger hung limp in his fingers. When Jackbird's father arrived, they left.

~

It was nearly dusk when Ned and his father got out of the truck at the same spot where they'd been picked up. His father began walking down the driveway, but Ned was made to linger on the road by something he saw in a near paddock. At first he thought the figure was a scarecrow, but then he saw that it was moving in a careful trudge.

He kept looking. The figure was slender and perhaps his height, although the distance made it hard to tell. A mane of straw-brown hair shook with each step the figure took—Callie. Jackbird's sister. She held a rake or a hoe, but was not dipping it to the earth. She just walked, her gait measured, back straight, face tilted to the sky. When she turned towards the road Ned saw she wasn't carrying a tool but a gun.

She didn't hold it the way he'd imagined; he'd thought there'd be a metallic sag to her march, the heft of the weapon obvious and uncomfortable in her arms. But in the flesh, in the ending of this afternoon, she appeared unburdened. The shotgun sat high and steady in her grip, and her strides spoke only of pride, concentration and—Ned imagined—vengeance.

~

That evening, after Ned had set his usual traps, he took a detour on his way back to the house. The image of Callie remained in his thoughts, vivid and unshakeable. Under the orange dusk he walked to the chicken coop and stopped at the patch Maggie had been inspecting that morning. On the grassless earth he set a trap, remembering his sister's words, the look on her face.

The twist of fire it had lit in him. He wondered how a hawk would be snared—if the bird would venture a talon first, or if it would thrust its sickle-beak forward, allowing the trap to crash through its tawny neck plumage to snap the hollow bones beneath. He went to sleep hot, sick with excitement and dread.

In the morning he resisted checking the coop trap first; he walked past it, rifle in hand, willing himself to hunt while hunting was optimal. Almost immediately he saw a rabbit grazing by a shallow creek that ran into the river. His bullet fetched it below the eye and flashed into its skull. A clean shot, an unmarred pelt: he thought it a good omen. But through the rest of the dawn he saw no more rabbits to aim at, and when he checked his traps they were all empty. He reset the triggered ones, shuffling them into more favourable positions on the grass. Only as he began walking home did he allow himself to visit the trap by the coop.

At first he thought it had failed. There was no dead bird, no pile of feathers shaken into the dirt. Yet as he got closer, he saw that the trap had been set off, and something else lay stuck in its jaws. Ned slowed. He tried to be silent, failed. A face whipped towards him.

The eyes sat above a long, heavily whiskered snout that ended in a pink nose. Small ears sat on the peak of the skull. The rest of the creature lay flat against the dirt, as if trying to diminish its appearance, although it couldn't hide the size of its torso, longer and larger than that of a house cat. Its rich brown fur, shining in the dawn, was splashed all over with bright cream-coloured spots. A thick tail, as long as head and body combined, flowed from its hindquarters, carrying more of the spots. Its legs were short, each ending in a clutch of long pink toes and curved claws.

Ned took another step. The quoll burst into a snarl, its jaws flying impossibly wide, revealing a mouth of white knives.

He had never seen one before. He'd heard talk of them—a small variety referred to as native cats, or larger ones like this called tiger cats—and knew them as poultry thieves, cannier and more vicious than even the red foxes of the empire. The only tangible evidence he'd had of their existence were the pelts he'd seen. One had been artfully stitched into a pencil case owned by one of his classmates; another was stretched across the back wall of Singline's shop. Uncommon treasures, spotted with brilliance.

Ned stared at the quoll, at its fur, at the snowy circles brightening the brownness. He'd get a good price for it—perhaps an outstanding one. Far more than he'd get for a rabbit pelt. Singline would know who to sell it to, if he didn't want to keep it as a partner for the one on his wall. He'd know people who'd pay good money for it, the sort of people who could turn it into one of those sleeveless garments wealthy ladies liked to pour over their shoulders.

Or he could give it to Maggie. He'd kill the pest, prise its colours free and present it to his sister as a gift. Not hawk feathers for her pillow, but a trophy nonetheless. Proof of his prowess, and a sign of how he could aid her. How talented he was.

His chest buzzed. *Oh great hunter.*

He laid his gun and rabbit on the ground, stepped forward, raising his left boot above the quoll. It reared back onto its hind legs, somehow widening its jaw even further, teeth needling the air. A deep, rasping scream sprang from its throat, tearing apart the morning's silence. It rose to the height of Ned's knee before, in an ugly movement, it fell.

Ned stopped. His boot hung high. The quoll hadn't landed on its front paws; it lay on its side, its body an awkward comma in the dirt. Soon it twisted around to rest its mouth on one of its hind legs.

Only then did Ned see that this was how the quoll had been caught: its rear right paw was held in the mouth of the trap. Blood had dried and matted around the wound from the metal teeth, crusting and darkening the quoll's fur. The ruby meat of the animal's flesh showed, as did dull stretches of tendon and blinks of bright bone. It must have tried to pull its leg free during the night, managing only to scrape itself open on the unyielding metal. Now, with Ned's boot above it, the quoll turned on itself, worrying at the rent material of its own leg. A pained chirrup leaked from the nipping teeth. Fresh blood dropped into the dirt.

Ned's boot was heavy. He felt a tremor in his balance. He wanted to put his foot back on the ground. He wanted, he realised, to stop the quoll from hurting itself. It was the pelt, he told himself: he wanted to stop it ruining the pelt. But as he watched it tear into itself, as he heard its rasping chirps of pain, he wasn't thinking of fur or money or Maggie. He just wanted to put an end to the scene before him.

But there was the matter of the quoll's teeth. Of its fear, its rage. Before he'd thought too hard about it he was marching to the apple shed, where he grabbed an empty wooden crate and the lid of a metal bin. Back at the coop he approached the creature and placed the crate over it. The quoll snapped and barked and writhed, but it couldn't reach Ned, nor could it escape the descending crate. When it was an inch off the ground Ned began sliding it away from the coop, feeling the quoll's body catch on the far side of the wood. The exposed trap began to drag along with it. He pushed down on the centre of the crate with his right hand, securing the animal within the box and leaving its ruined leg and the trap outside. Higher, louder screams revealed how this heightened the quoll's pain, but it allowed Ned to use his free left hand to lever open the trap and unglue the bloody paw from its fangs.

He threw the trap onto the grass and pressed the injured paw through the gap between the crate and the ground. The screams had stopped. He grabbed the metal lid and slowly slid it underneath the crate, allowing the quoll to climb onto it as he used it to seal the aperture. With the sun now round in the sky he carried the crate to the shed, upended it in a dark nook behind a stack of other crates and weighed the lid down with two bricks. He did not allow himself to think; he retrieved his gun and the rabbit he'd shot earlier, and went to breakfast.

# 5

THE QUOLL FOLLOWED him for years, its jaw gaping through his mind whenever he found terror and fury in the same place. It came to him when he watched a boy throw a rock at his mother in the main street of Beaconsfield. When, in a pub after a football match, he saw two drunk ruckmen brutalise each other on the whorled grains of a myrtle table. When he was rouseabouting on the hell-hot sheep stations of the mainland, and witnessed overheated kelpies turn froth-mouthed and savage. And once, when he was twenty, close to home.

He was northwest of Limberlost, floating through a patch of sea that lay off a coastline busy with cliffs, coves and dry forests. With him were Jackbird and some other friends from the valley, including a young woman who'd lately been distracting Ned at all hours of the day, even when he wasn't near her. They had driven to where the road ended, before walking across the cliffs, through thick stands of she-oaks and scratching bracken, until the track fell down a slope and ran to a narrow inlet. This hidden cove was bordered by steep walls of craggy dolerite. Beyond it, the ocean gathered in a vast, shining plain.

Ned was snorkelling over a reef, looking for abalone. Blacklips were abundant here—their swirling, rust-patterned shells disguised among the weed and rock, but eventually discernible if you stared hard enough. Fish flicked across the reef, mostly grey-yellow wrasse, but also toadfish, orange gurnard, banded morwong. Every now and then Ned spotted the shifting pattern of a cuttlefish, tickling through the weed. Where the rocks gave way to pale seafloor there were schools of cocky salmon, flitting just below the surface. Beneath them, huge black discs glided across the sand: hunting skates, their barbs trailing on long tails behind them.

Down to this reef Ned dived. His eyes moved fast, skittering across the weeds, the textures, the splashes of colour that crusted the rocks. Soon his lungs began to tighten, and he was forced to resurface. The Letteremairrener women who lived on this coast would dive for long stretches of time, filling woven bags they carried around their necks with as many abalone as they could find. He'd heard the old people of the valley talk about them, the ones who remembered such things. Ned could only stay underwater for a single minute. When he felt the urgent burn for air he thought of those native women, smeared warm by seal fat, prising shell after shell free with clever wooden chisels. He could barely capture one at a time, and used a rusty flathead screwdriver to do it. A hollowness echoed through him when he made these comparisons; he became aware of his lack of skill, his dearth of lessons, of old knowledge. He felt the looseness of his connection to the place. How tenuous his grip on the world was.

But the sun was high, the water still. He took in more air to dive again. Soon he saw the domed, speckled shape of an abalone in the blue murk. He kicked downwards, trying to stay in position as he slid the screwdriver's blade beneath the lip of the shell. Sometimes the animal felt these attentions and suckered onto its perch, becoming harder to remove; multiple dives would be required to wedge it off. But this time Ned was quick: he speared the screwdriver in against the rock and flicked the abalone loose before it sensed him. The shell floated free, and as he grasped it he saw a shift of mottled colour, close to his hand.

It didn't zip away like most fish would. Nor did it bob and waft like a squid or cuttlefish. Ned resurfaced, gulped air, went back down. At first he saw only reef and water, but then it happened again—the nervous retreat of blue-brown texture behind a flat, vertical rock. He swam forward, and saw the truth of it: a large leatherjacket.

It faced Ned, huddled against the rock. The spine on its forehead had risen, and the fish had angled its body to point this weapon at its pursuer. The thing was more like a horn than a spine—the leatherjacket a small aquatic unicorn.

Ned floated before it. He'd only ever seen these fish as by-catch. They were hauled in foul-hooked, no fight in their flesh, and spat loud grunts as they flapped against jetties and decks. He'd thought them senseless, pointless creatures. But this water-cloaked leatherjacket was thrumming with fearful energy. Its horn-spine rose higher. Its body shimmied with tightly held power. Its mouth opened, showing a row of teeth.

That was when the quoll and the chicken coop found their way back to him. The leatherjacket's defences shot them into his mind. The quoll cornered, rearing. Its spots so bright in the morning light, its wound-blood and dark fur and glinting bone. Its mouth erupting with hissing screams and shining teeth. Its fury. Its panic.

Ned's chest burned, half with a need for air, half with something else, crimson and heavy. The fish lunged towards him. He kicked up to the surface.

When he broke the sea's skin he gasped, sucking air. He wiped his eyes, blinking at the salt, the sunlight. The abalone he'd levered free was still in his hand; he was surprised to see it there, the pucker of its muscle squirming in his palm.

As he reoriented himself to this drier, heavier world he looked back to the cove and saw the young woman who'd been distracting him of late. She was lying on the rocks, framed by the high cliffs, a hand raised to guard her eyes from the light, and then Ned was not thinking of teeth or fear but only of the sun, the heat, her skin.

# 6

DAYS OF DRYNESS followed Ned's capture of the quoll. The wind warmed, then died. The sun bit and clawed. Mud hardened into dirt, before falling apart as dust. Sweat crusted onto skin as soon as it leaked free. New, thirsty growth hung low on the apple trees; Ned's father dug furrows in the orchard, hoping any spare moisture would run down onto the roots. All over the valley the grass shook off its spring-grown greenness and collapsed into yellow slumber. With no freshness to feed on, the rabbits disappeared.

The only joy to be found was in the arms of the river. Each afternoon, after their fathers dismissed them, Ned and Jackbird would make for a pebbly beach not far from Limberlost's northern boundary. They'd take their rods in case they encountered anyone they needed to impress—fishing being a nobler pursuit than swimming—but never come close to baiting a hook. At the beach they'd kick off their boots, peel off their shirts and wince over the burning stones into the water, dousing their work-hot skin in the waves.

They'd stroke out over the shallows, towards the distant eastern shore. When they reached a depth the height of their necks they'd use their skulls to crack open the surface, and once fully submerged they would upend their bodies, kicking downwards, thrusting themselves to the one place it was truly cold: the riverbed. Only then would they stop moving. Only in the low, cooling current would they allow themselves to relax. Only there, beneath the river's shining ceiling, would Ned let himself remember the creature in his father's shed.

~

He hadn't told anyone about the quoll. He behaved as if his summer was unchanged, as if the capture hadn't taken place. He swam with Jackbird. He helped his father shepherd the apples towards autumn. When Maggie puzzled over the unmolested chicken coop, he looked at the trees. Each morning he took up his rifle and checked his traps, although the scarcity of rabbits meant he had little success. The few he killed were the smallest he'd seen all season, and their pelts were dull. He cut the skins free anyway, hanging them in the shed as he normally would. Afterwards—once he'd checked that Maggie and his father were not watching—he carved flecks of stringy meat off the naked corpses and gave them, piece by piece, to the quoll.

Feeding was a dangerous, unpredictable process. Ned could never know how the quoll would react to him. Inching the bin lid open usually summoned the creature upwards, its teeth flashing and snapping at the aperture, and he could do nothing but jam in slivers of meat before hurriedly resealing the gap. Other times it lay still, regarding him with benign curiosity, and he could remove the lid entirely, offer hunks of rabbit to its snout, and wait for the quoll to deftly snatch them from his shaking fingers.

Occasionally it was asleep, and he could watch its snow-patterned torso shift with the air that came in and out of it. In these moments he studied the delicacy of its face, the bunched strength in its neck and shoulders, the curling length of its tail, the shape of its lithe body. It became a marvellous thing, beautiful and impossible. A demon from a sharper world. He avoided looking at its savaged leg.

Sometimes it let him dip a hand near its face, only to hiss and snap at his fingers. Sometimes it screamed. Sometimes it bashed against the walls of the crate the moment it heard him approaching, its furious barks rasping through the shed, and he did not risk feeding it at all.

He knew he shouldn't be keeping it. Its pelt was worth more than his boots. Its wound was a scene of carnage. He should kill it, for mercy as much as for money. And even if its leg somehow healed, if he somehow nursed the quoll to health and set it free, it would not abandon its instincts or its hunger. It would return to the chicken coop, find a way under the wire, smash open the eggs and slaughter the flapping mothers, ripping at flesh and feathers with ancient, efficient violence. Blood would drench the straw. Maggie would wake to the carcasses.

He hadn't thought about the boat for days.

~

When the heat broke Maggie asked Ned if he wanted to go riding. He didn't like horses—huge, storm-mouthed creatures that had huffed terror into him when he was younger. The jitter in their necks, in their eyes, despite their size and muscle. He'd never believed that they wouldn't kick or throw him. One of the first times he'd climbed onto a horse it had laid a fierce bite on his upper arm. Each winter he could feel its jaw through his flesh—a ghost clamping on the hardness of his bone.

No one else in his family shared his fear. His mother, he'd been told, had loved them so much she'd thought of them as friends. His father had grown up on farms where horses mattered as much as rain, and had never abandoned this idea of their importance. He'd also been part of a cavalry regiment, although when asked about it all he'd say was that horses weren't made for modern warfare. Bill had been the best rider in the district—a fact Ned accepted, as he did all of Bill's talents, without question. Asking his eldest brother where his skills came from wouldn't have been any use, anyway; Bill would just have ridden off. Toby hadn't been particularly interested in horses, but when he discovered the effect of galloping at full pelt through the district on a Saturday afternoon—when the local girls and young women were out visiting each other—it became hard to prise him from whichever animal would let him onto its back.

But it was Maggie who had loved them most. She was up with them every morning before the rest of the family woke. She brushed them, fed them, walked them, checked them, rode them, spoke to them, disciplined them, sang to them, prayed for them, closed her eyes and, in frosted dawns and muggy dusks, wordlessly communed with them. It was an unwritten law of the orchard that the horses belonged to Maggie, even if she held no specific right of ownership over them. To take one out meant speaking with her first. To walk in the light of her favour required doing something considerate for a horse: to bring one an apple, to tweezer off its ticks.

Ned couldn't ride like Bill, couldn't dash and smile like Toby. When he saw a horse he saw only the spook in its nature, felt only the stallion's yellow teeth on his arm. So when Maggie asked if he wanted to go riding, Ned said no. He had chores to take care of, he told her. Fruit to check, rabbits to skin, weeds to pull.

She looked at him. Waited a moment. 'I suppose I'll find somebody else.'

She walked away, her back straight, her stride long. He pictured her riding with Bill, the two of them cresting a stubbled hill, Bill trailing to give her the lead. Ned knew, too late, that he'd failed her—failed her in the way he'd sworn not to when she'd returned to the orchard.

~

Later that day he tried to clean out the quoll's crate. He'd done this a few times before, and it had never gone well. It involved slowly lifting the crate, sliding off the lid, then tipping the contents, quoll included, into another crate that he hastily lidded and weighted. He'd clean out the dirty crate and fill it with fresh straw before decanting his struggling, shrieking prisoner back into it. The procedure always made a lot of mess, and the shed would be filled with sounds of unholy rage. Always he was sure Maggie or his father would hear.

This time he found the quoll asleep. Deciding to try his luck, he pulled on a pair of thick gloves and slid his fingers beneath its softly heaving torso. It didn't react, not even when he

gently raised it into the air and draped it into the spare box. He
cleaned the crate as quickly as he could and turned back to find
the quoll still sleeping. He lifted it again, gingerly, glacially. It was
only when he lowered it onto the clean straw that it woke. A set
of heavy blinks tricked Ned into thinking that sleep had rendered
it woozy and slow; an instant later it had twisted in his grip,
squirming to clamp its jaws onto his glove. Hot teeth daggered
through the stiff fabric, lancing into the meat of his palm. He
swore and dropped the quoll into the crate. It fell, screaming and
barking from the moment its mouth detached from Ned's flesh.
He barely managed to replace the lid before it clawed its way out.
The sounds of its fury echoed through the shed.

Ned ripped the glove from his hand. Blood ran from two
shallow punctures near the base of his thumb. He wiped the
wounds on his leg. The crate rattled. He thought about kicking
it. Turned to leave. Saw someone in the entrance. Felt panic rip
through him, and just managed to hold in a cry.

It was Jackbird's sister, Callie. Her body was framed by
the light that came through the doorway, her hair thick with
the sun's glint. She was staring past him, into the depths of the
shed. Ned thought she looked different, an incorrect version of
herself. He hadn't spoken to her since before the last school year
had started. Five months. Maybe longer.

After a dry stutter, he found his voice. 'What are you doing
here?'

'A lot less than you, it seems.'

'I'm just tidying some things up.'

A throaty hiss rumbled from behind Ned's legs. He shifted
in front of the crate.

Callie looked past him. 'Your sister invited me to go riding.'

Ned pointed out the door. 'Stables are that way.'

'Already been there. Your mare is limping.'

For a second, Ned forgot the quoll. Imagined Maggie discovering a horse's wound. 'Shit.'

'Your sister is talking to your dad about it. She's not happy.'

'I'll bet.'

Ned crossed his arms, looked for something to lean on. Callie kept staring, showed no sign of leaving.

'Was on my way home when I heard some animal being murdered.'

'It's just me in here.'

'And whatever you've got in that apple crate.'

Ned felt heat in his cheeks, and hoped the dimness of the shed would hide the colour from her. 'I was skinning a rabbit. Turned out it wasn't completely dead. That's what you heard.'

'You skun a living creature?'

'No. Yep. Not deliberately.'

'Show me what's in the crate.'

'You never a seen a rabbit?'

She folded her arms, mirroring Ned's posture. Blew a breath out her nose. 'Guess I'll just go tell Maggie you're skinning rabbits alive. And that you're keeping something secret up here. And that you rode her horse into a rabbit trap. And that...'

'All right, all right. Jesus.'

Ned stepped back from the crate. His face was still hot; he couldn't think of a bluff or excuse; he felt in his whole body the mistake of it all. But he was wedged. She was walking forward. He inched the lid off the crate, giving her room to peek in.

'Don't touch it.'

She leaned over the gap. Ned stayed tense, waiting for the quoll to explode upwards, to claw the skin off her bony knuckles, her narrow wrists. Nothing happened. Callie looked for a long time.

'That a tiger cat?'

'A quoll.'

'It's hurt.'

'I trapped it.' Saying it filled him with guilt. 'Accident.'

She straightened up, still staring into the crate. Hair wisped away from the base of her head. Ned noticed these tawny strands escaping the grip of her hairband, then looked down, remembering the danger of the quoll. It had curled in on itself and was licking its injured foot. The wound had turned a claret colour, glistening and hard. Its pink tongue worried at the nugs of dried blood that had scabbed over the exposed flesh.

Callie glanced at him. 'You know they kill chickens.'

'So I've heard.'

Ned remembered seeing her with the shotgun, remembered what Jackbird had told him about her relentless pursuit of the hawk. He waited for her to tell him to kill it. To try to kill it herself. If she reached into the crate with death in her mind, with a knife in her hand, he didn't know what he'd do. He didn't know if he'd do anything at all.

But all she did was turn to him. 'What are you going to do with it?'

'I don't know.'

Her eyes narrowed. 'Does Jackbird know?'

'No. No one does.'

Something like satisfaction drew itself across her face. She looked back into the crate, drawn to the quoll. Ned knew the feeling. The tug of its wildness.

'Don't tell him. Or anyone else. Please.'

Callie was still staring. 'Look at it.'

Ned peered into the crate. The quoll wasn't doing anything notable; it was just breathing, licking, twitching its nose and whiskers. The circles of cream on its fur had dulled and dirtied. Occasionally it looked up at them; whiteless eyes snagging on their own.

They lingered a few minutes, hooked on the animal, before Callie said she had chores to do. She agreed to not say anything to her brother. After she left Ned went inside to rub iodine on the holes the quoll had put in his hand. The copper liquid stung at the meat of him.

~

Maggie's wrath hit the orchard like heavy hail. Ned and his father had never experienced anything like it. At any moment she was liable to stop what she was doing and accuse them of laziness, of carelessness, of slug-minded stupidity. Letting a horse become injured was bad enough, but to do nothing about it? To not even notice? Ned was a child, she spat, smart enough to kill wild animals but too thick to care for one already tamed. Their father, on the other hand, was a garden-variety fool. She could barely look at them. More heat blazed in her than in all the months of summer.

Ned felt this blame—at least the part she'd apportioned to him—was unfair. He didn't go near the horses: the whole family knew that. How was he to know one had hurt itself? But perhaps that was his sister's point. Still, he felt poorly treated.

When she rounded on him over lunch two days after she'd discovered the limp, saying that Bill would never have let a horse walk wounded, that even Toby would have done something about it, he left the kitchen without responding.

Outside, a breeze that had touched the river rose to cool the blood in his cheeks. Knowing his father would be in the far paddock, he made for the shed, thinking he'd check on the quoll, feed it earlier than usual. Inside he pulled on the thick gloves, tore off a twist of half-dried rabbit meat from a hanging carcass, teased open the lid of the crate and dipped the food into the gloom. He hovered, tense, waiting for the quoll's jaw to snatch at the meat. No teeth rose. No sound.

He removed the lid completely, letting the subdued light wash the crate's interior. Inside he saw the creature lying curled and still. Its eyes were closed. There was a stiffness to it that he hadn't seen before; for a moment he thought it was dead. Then he saw movement—short, uneven breaths that played a ripple across the quoll's torso.

He placed the meat near its jaw. It gave no indication that it noticed. Ned stood there, watching the quoll's harried breaths, feeling himself swell with panic. He suddenly felt that Maggie was right in everything she'd said about him. When he was able to look away he placed a second piece of rabbit flesh in the crate, then left, almost running.

That night, after he had gone to bed, he heard his father and Maggie talking.

'At least take her to the vet,' she was saying.

'Not an option. You know that.'

44

'The limp will get worse.'

'She might shake it off.'

'More likely she'll go permanently lame and we'll have to shoot her.'

'Possibly.'

'And that doesn't worry you?'

Ned heard a hard sigh push through the house's boards. 'Choices aren't thick on the ground, Magpie.'

'You could get Ned to do the shooting. He wouldn't mind.'

'That's enough.'

'Mum would—'

'Don't.'

A chair scraped, hard enough to dig scratches into the floor. A door closed. A tap ran. Lying on his summer sheets Ned felt the panic and loathing that had come to him in the shed return, fizzing through his body, burning up his stillness. He could not sleep for all the trouble in his head.

# 7

THE NEXT MORNING he did not go shooting. He did not check his traps. With the sky still stained purple by the dawn he marched to the stables, where he cooed at the injured mare until she ceased jittering and let him dress her with a saddle and bridle. As he led her to the driveway he saw how pronounced her limp was, so he walked slowly, letting the mare set the pace. He told himself that she was a sorry, damaged thing. That she wasn't a stallion.

Before he left the orchard he tethered the horse by the shed, went inside and grabbed the quoll's crate. He couldn't find the strength to look into it. Instead he wrapped an old strap around its top and base, knotted it tight and carried it outside, where he secured it to the saddle with another strap. He shook the crate, checking to see that its movements were not too severe. When he was content, they continued.

They made it down the driveway and out onto the road without being detected. Soon they crested the hills nearest the river, passing the two-room primary school he and Jackbird had attended together. A tall, wide-limbed oak leaned over the weatherboard building, heavy with foliage, picture-book verdant against the blond paddocks and blue-green stretch of eucalypts and paperbarks that ran down to the water. No one had yet thought to cut these natives down and plant a European orchard—the land was too rugged, the trees too dense. Even in these early hours they leaked their summer oils, shimmering the air, thickening the light.

On Ned and the mare walked, staying to the side of the gravel road. Morning wallabies sprang away from them into the trees and bracken. Near the shore the forest had been peeled back to make way for houses, mostly small cottages and fishing shacks, although Ned knew that one long maple-lined driveway led to a convent not visible from the road.

Early one Sunday morning Toby had torn up to its entrance on horseback, hoping to throw some colour into the young ladies of the Lord, before being chased back to Limberlost by a pair of black-brown Dobermans. He'd arrived home sweating and scared—more, Ned had been able to tell, of their father's reaction than the dogs. Ned didn't know if Toby had been riding the same horse he now led past the convent driveway. The mare did not show any sign of fear or familiarity.

Down the road fell, past the final reaches of forest, to run alongside the water. Small boats and yachts were tethered to pastel buoys. Ned stared at them and felt his heart prickle. The tide was out, and the exposed shore squirmed with crabs, twisting themselves into the damp sand. They passed the jetty where he and Jackbird fished. The mare paused, taking the weight off her bad leg. Ned rubbed her flank, tried to be gentle, and told her in a soft trill that they did not have far to go.

He'd only visited the vet once, six summers earlier, but he remembered that her surgery, which was also her home, lay in a wet elbow of the valley by a crooked stream. On that first visit he'd been with Jackbird and his father, taking a snake-bitten kelpie for treatment. The boys had found the dog near a frog pond, snarling and frothing at the huge black-backed tiger. They'd fetched Jackbird's father, who pulled the dog into the yard and decapitated the snake with a spade with the same emotion a man might show when buttering toast. After burying the snake's head he saw how his son and Ned had crowded around the dog, which had lain down, foam bubbling from its mouth. Jackbird had insisted on accompanying his father to the vet, had dragged Ned along with him.

Ned remembered how sure he'd been that the kelpie would recover. Jackbird had been so confident—the vet knew how to treat snakebites, he'd said, easy as pissing, and that confidence had flowed into Ned. Later, he realised that Jackbird had been filled with the boyish rush of witnessing his father's bravery and violence. In a moment like that anything seemed possible— steadfast men would save loyal friends, wise doctors would heal grave wounds. At the vet's the boys had waited outside as his father carried the dog in. Minutes later they heard the bark of a rifle.

Of the vet, Ned saw only a tall, trousered woman emerging from the surgery, watching as Jackbird's father dumped the dead kelpie into the tray of the utility. On the way home the body slid with each corner, thumping into the sides of the tray with fleshy weight. It was this memory that came to Ned clearest: the sound of the dog's corpse smacking at the metal, and how much it had troubled him to see Jackbird crying beside him in the cab. How he'd looked away from his friend, stared hard at the gums rushing past the window.

~

Ned and the mare approached the vet's house. It was an old cottage built with large sandstone blocks. A rust-hazed corrugated iron extension had been tacked onto the back. He wasn't sure how to approach—the front door, as manners dictated, or through the rear of the property, which made more sense with a horse in tow. The mare huffed at his side.

'Help you?'

The vet had walked out from behind the iron extension. Ned didn't fully recognise her, but she was tall and grey and wore battered trousers, and that's all he remembered about the woman he'd seen the day the kelpie had died.

He raised a hand. 'Good morning.'

'It is.'

Ned pointed at the horse's bad leg. 'She's got a limp.'

'Does she now.'

'Yes.'

'Let's have a look.'

Ned wasn't sure what the vet meant until she raised a finger and ran it back and forth through the air. He pulled on the bridle, leading the mare up the road, then took her back. When the vet remained silent he did it again, and again, labouring the mare over the gravel.

'Better bring her through.'

When he turned, the vet was walking around the extension, her back to him. He followed, coaxing the mare along.

Behind the house was a dense garden, plotted with dark-soiled patches of vegetables. Asymmetrical paths curled through the leafy beds. Tomato vines climbed a far lattice. Where the garden ended the bush appeared, thick and insistent, a mix of she-oaks, black gums and ferns, rising up the slope to form a greenish amphitheatre. The stream he remembered from his previous visit zigzagged through the trees.

To the left of the garden was an open shed, packed with what Ned assumed were items of veterinary equipment, as well as ordinary tools and gardening paraphernalia. The vet was standing beside it, on the only patch of unworked dirt in the yard. She beckoned him, impatience in the snap of her wrist. He led the horse to her side and unfastened the crate, placing it on the ground beside a shock of carrot sprouts.

The vet touched the mare's nose. When it steadied she peeled back its lips, studied the wetness of its eyes, paused a hand on each of its flanks. She gazed into its ears. She combed her fingers through its mane. Finally, she walked behind it to lift and bend its bad leg.

'Fetch that,' she said, pointing at a stump. Ned lifted it, struggled with the weight, heaved it over to her. She placed the mare's raised foot on its surface and began studying the flat side of the hoof.

'You're William West's youngest. From Limberlost.'

'Yes, that's right. I'm Ned.'

She gazed at the base of the hoof. The mare's fetlock shook, but otherwise she was still. 'There's an impaction here,' said the vet. 'Get my chisel.'

She held out a hand. Ned fumbled into the shed, cast around for a veterinary chisel. He found an ordinary one, rusted and heavy. It seemed wrong, but he picked it up and handed it to the vet, who immediately turned it on the hoof.

Thick curls of dirty keratin rolled up from the gouging blade. The vet was attacking a deep groove in the centre of the hoof, furrowing in from a range of angles. More dead material peeled away, littering the garden like a whittler's shavings. After a minute the vet stopped, stared at her work, placed the chisel on the ground.

'Screwdriver. Flathead.'

Ned found one, this time not hesitating. The vet wedged it hard into the hoof and began applying force to the handle. The shaft of the screwdriver bent beneath her strength. She twisted, repositioned. Again the metal bowed. The vet grunted. The mare shook. To Ned, the world seemed paused in this moment of quiet pressure, as if the forest and garden were holding them still. Then a grating pop cut the air, the screwdriver snapped back into rigidity, and something flew from the hoof to land by the carrots.

Ned watched it hit the soil: a shard of rock half the size of his thumb. A dark liquid glossed its contours. As he watched light wink off its surface, a foulness rushed into his nostrils. A thick and fatty waft of rot. He flinched, staring at the shard, wondering at the horror of it, at how it could leak such poison into the air. It was only when he turned to the vet that he realised the rock wasn't the source of the scent.

Twin currents of blood and pus were coursing from a

ragged hole in the mare's hoof, mixing into a thin red-yellow rivulet that dripped down and spattered the stump beneath the fetlock. Ned could taste it—the rich, glistening flavour of infection. Bile streamed up his throat. He looked away, sucked on forest air. When he felt surer of his stomach, he turned back and saw the vet swabbing at the rotted hoof with a cloth she'd dipped in iodine.

Through all of this, the mare had stayed more or less still. It allowed the vet to clean the wound and patch it with a kind of tar or glue Ned did not recognise.

When the vet was happy with her work she stood up and lowered the hoof to the ground. She coaxed the mare into taking a gentle step forward. Once the horse was steady, she patted its neck and returned her chisel, screwdriver, cloth and bottle of iodine to the shed.

Ned waited for the vet to remember he was there. When she gave no sign of it, he spoke up.

'Is that it?

'She'll need a few weeks of rest.'

'Will she live?'

The mare had begun grazing on the nearby grass. The vet rubbed her hands on her trousers. 'She will unless you kill her.'

Ned thanked her. He retrieved the stump and returned it to its original spot in the garden. Then he walked to the mare, watched her eat, tried to let gladness fill him. Tried to imagine how Maggie's face would look when he told her. What she'd say about what he had done here.

With his sister's expression fixed in his mind, he found that he had the courage to raise the thing he'd been avoiding.

'There's something else.'

The vet let his statement hang, gave him room in her garden to explain himself. When he did not—for his courage had died in the chill of her silence—she indicated the crate he'd brought with an angled neck. 'You're referring to that.'

'I am.'

She waited a moment longer—just long enough for Ned to think she was going to turn him away—before she pointed to a workbench in the open shed. Ned lifted the crate and carefully placed it on the surface. He began removing the straps. Straightaway he wanted to stop; he wanted to take the crate and leave, to go home, to keep hiding it in his father's shed, answer no questions and face no consequences, and continue his summer of lonesome killing in peace.

But the vet was waiting, and her silence was beginning to overwhelm him. He undid the straps, removed the lid, stepped back from the crate. The vet moved forward, looked inside. Ned stared at her garden, at the grazing mare. When he could stare no longer he looked back at the vet. She was still engaged with the crate's contents. Her face remained impassive until she finally spoke. 'You trap it?'

'I did.'

She straightened up. 'On purpose?'

'No.' He nearly told her about the hawk, about Callie's chickens. But he realised immediately how foolish it would make him seem—how it would reveal the lack of thought that had resulted in the quoll's wounding—so he added nothing else.

The vet did not ask for a further explanation. Neither, to

Ned's relief, did she ask what he intended to do with it, why he hadn't killed it. She just dipped slow hands into the crate, positioned them carefully, and lifted the quoll out onto a blanket. It was limp in her grip.

Ned clenched his teeth, sucked his tongue. He noticed the lethargy in its body, the darkness of its wound. The weakness in its breathing.

The vet lifted the damaged leg. The quoll was awake, but it did not move to bite or stop her. She inspected the blooded fur, the exposed flesh. 'You've done some damage to this fellow.'

She took a small knife from a leather bag on the bench. Ned felt panicked, felt sick. But the vet only used the blade to push back the fur so she could see the torn flesh in greater detail. She ran her eyes over the extent of the injury, sometimes moving her face so close to the wound that her nose brushed fur and scabs. Once she had finished inspecting the rent leg she began looking over the rest of the quoll. She placed a firm hand on the back of its neck, then leaned in to see its eyes, its small, neat ears. She put the knife back in the bag and placed a finger on its neck, feeling for the rhythm of its heart.

At no point did the quoll react to her attentions. If anything, Ned thought, the creature kept its dark eyes on him.

'What have you been feeding it?'

'Rabbit.'

'Rabbits eating your old man's apples, are they? Strange rabbits up your way.'

He reddened. 'I'm selling the pelts. Army uses them for hats.'

'You caught many?'

'Plenty.'

'And one harmless tiger cat.'

Her tone did not invite a response. A minute later she asked him to wet a cloth under the garden tap. When he returned, her hand was still on the quoll's neck but she had retrieved a roll of gauze from somewhere. He handed her the cloth, and she began to wipe and excavate the wound. The quoll squirmed, but it did not have the strength to fight her grip.

'So you're making money.'

'I suppose.'

'And I take it you'll use that money to pay me for whatever I can do for this fellow?'

'And for fixing my sister's mare. All of it.'

She turned to place her flat eyes on his. 'Maybe, Ned West. Maybe.' Her hand remained pressed on the quoll's back. 'But you haven't been selling pelts to pay for a horse that's only just gone lame.'

She began dabbing iodine at the wound, much less than she'd put on the mare's hoof. At the sting of the antiseptic the quoll began to jerk. It twisted its neck, snapping at the vet's hand, but it couldn't reach. High, outraged hissing spat from its mouth. When the vet began to massage the meat of the wound, to rearrange the torn flesh into a neater position over the exposed bone, the hisses rose into screams, harsher than any sound Ned had heard the quoll make before. It seemed impossible for a creature of such slightness and beauty to create a sound so violent.

Ned felt his fingers trembling, his face, his thighs. He turned away, gave himself back to the leafy textures of the garden.

When the screams ceased, he looked back. The quoll was again motionless, and the vet was wrapping gauze around the wound. After three loops around the limb she tied the material off and let her grip on the quoll loosen. It was shaking. When it did not try to run or escape, she turned to him.

'What were you saving for?'

Ned was watching the quoll shiver. 'Sorry?'

'The money you're going to pay me with. What were you going to do with it?'

'Just saving.'

'Strange thing to do. Come here asking favours. Telling lies.'

Ned stared at her. 'I said I'll pay you.'

'Not what I asked.'

'I was going to give it to my father. Help out.'

'I know your old man. He won't take your money.'

'Why do you care?'

'Why are you lying?'

'I want a boat.'

The vet smiled, and there was a curl of sadness on her lips. Or perhaps it was the shape of understanding. 'Of course you do.'

Ned's thoughts were swarming. It had been so simple: a bit of pressure, and his secret was revealed. He swore at himself. Within him there was a gurgling churn, in his throat and his organs and his pulse. He couldn't face what he'd told her, couldn't acknowledge what he'd revealed. He scrabbled at his pocket, tinkling his fingers through the mess of coins he'd brought.

'How much?'

Still the vet smiled. 'I don't want your bunny money, lad. You can pay me with labour.'

Ned looked around the shed. Took in the instruments of her work. 'I don't even know how to shoe a horse.'

'I don't want an assistant.' She gestured at her garden. 'I have a rabbit problem. Can't plant a thing without them eating every shoot. Can't keep them out. I have no traps, and no inclination to get up before sunrise and tramp around blasting a gun at them.' The vet, still with an arm on the quoll, pointed to the fence at the end of her garden. 'You come and knock off fifty or so rabbits. That should do for the mare and your friend here.'

Shrewdness calmed Ned's mind. 'Can I keep the pelts?'

'I'm not fussed what you do with them. Buy your boat. Buy a fleet. As long as my garden grows.'

Her smile lingered, before skewing off her mouth as she looked back down at the bandaged creature. She indicated the crate with her chin. Ned grabbed it, shook out the straw and muck. The vet lifted the trembling quoll and put it in the crate. Ned fastened the lid. The vet rested a hand on its surface.

'Feed him duck eggs, if you can. You'll know when he's right to be released. He'll get lively and start ripping off your fingers.' She flexed her hands and walked into the garden's light. Ned lifted the crate and followed her.

'Thank you.'

She gave him a slight nod. 'The horse needs rest. Leave her with me. I'll let you know when you she's ready to go home.' She moved to the mare, ran an eye over the line of its neck. 'Lucky your brothers aren't around to ride her into the knackery.'

It was late morning when Ned made it back to the orchard. The weather was warm but not oppressive. The rows of apple trees ran before him in a healthy grid, their clawing branches heavy with young fruit. He felt light and good. He'd convinced himself that his accidental confession didn't matter, because the vet, being a near-hermit, surely wouldn't tell anyone. His boat dreams would remain a secret. And he had a new source of rabbits—garden-fed, lustrous and fat. And the quoll would live, and so would the mare, and he was the one who had done it: he, and only he, had fixed these things.

His arms were sore and the crate heavy as he returned it to the shed. Before he left he peeked beneath the lid. Inside the quoll was asleep. Its breathing seemed normal, and Ned chose to believe that it was not in pain, that it was peacefully regaining its strength after the ordeal of the vet's attentions. He wondered how he would get his hands on duck eggs, then left the shed and went down to the house.

Inside he found Maggie, bent over a piece of paper in the hallway. He wanted to tell her what he'd done. He wanted shock to bloom on her face, shock that would swim into joy. He wanted her to loose praise in his direction. But as he moved into the house he noticed how fiercely she studied the paper in her hands.

'What's that?'

Maggie looked up. When she saw that it was him her eyes returned to the paper. 'Letter.'

'Who from?'

'None of your business.' Her voice was quick. She folded the letter. 'A friend. He's in the north. As far north as you can get. He's stationed on a ship, keeping the passage to Russia clear. It's so cold that every night ice freezes to the sides of the boat. Huge sheets of it. You don't really think of ice as heavy, do you, but all this ice slows the ship down. And it's a hazard, and makes the structure top-heavy, apparently. So each morning, as soon as he wakes up, he's hoisted up the side of this great metal ship with a sledgehammer to bash apart these enormous sheets of ice. It's so cold he can't feel his face, but up he goes, walloping away, and down comes the ice, sharp as glass, smashing to pieces on the deck. He says that afterwards he can't tell if his fingers are numb from the cold or from the hammer reverberating in his hands. Every morning. They dock in Murmansk. Imagine that. Murmansk.'

She was looking towards him again, but Ned felt that her eyes were trained not on his face but somewhere else. He didn't know what to say. He thought he should ask for this friend's name, how they met, but at the same time those questions felt intrusive and inappropriate. He turned the word Murmansk over in his mind.

Maggie pointed to the small table near the doorway. 'You've got one too.'

'What?'

'A letter.'

He looked at the table. On it, amid keys and knives and dust, he saw an envelope. He picked it up, and saw in its design the indicators of military correspondence. The air in the hall became uncomfortable. He ripped the envelope open. Forgot about his sister, about the mare, the morning. Unfolded the letter within, took it out into the near-noon light.

*Ned,*

*You can stop drenching the orchard with your tears. I am alive and well. We are still yet to deploy. I haven't even fired my rifle, other than at birds. I'm the best shot in the Pacific, although there are no girls around to see it, so it's a waste of bullets.*

*I'm not allowed to tell you where we are stationed in case this letter is intercepted. But it is hot and dull and the ocean is all around. The food would not be considered legal back home. Sometimes the air-raid sirens go off, but so far they've all been false alarms. There have been no attacks in months. I thought this would be many things but I did not imagine it would be so boring. I have met some terrific fellows, though.*

*They say it will all be finished soon. It seems unlikely that you'll be called up. Typical of your luck. It also seems unlikely I will see any action at all. Be sure to tell everyone that I'm a war hero regardless.*

*Has Bill written? The last I heard, his division had been routed from Singapore, although that was a long time ago. Good thing he can shoot nearly as well as I can. It's not as if he'll be charming the enemy into surrendering.*

*Be good to Dad and if Maggie is there do what she tells you. I know I never did but I suppose I should have.*
*Toby*

# 8

COULD IT HAVE been Toby who gave him the coat that night at the river mouth? Even though he was on the other side of the boat? The thought bit into Ned's mind at the base of a raging waterfall, years after reading his brother's letter.

Ned had returned from the mainland six months earlier, after two years working on the great cattle and sheep stations of the interior. Soon after arriving home he drove to the birthday party of a second cousin, on a farm three valleys over from Limberlost. This valley's river was narrow, full of twists, highland-fed. Dark freshwater, prone to swelling after winter rains that were predictable enough to allow for dairy farming, the huge and defining industry of the place. No orchards in sight. No trees other than lonesome gums kept alive for stock shelter. Dairy farms patterned every stitch of flat land, right up to the steep tiers that bordered the workable soil. Black-white cows speckled every paddock.

Ned expected drinks, speeches—a sense of familiarity, of

reunion. Other attendees had different ideas. It was autumn, and the ground was not yet drenched, and among the young men at the party there was a contagious desire to burn things. A bonfire was called for, then multiple bonfires—a competition was suggested, where two groups would fight to see who could build a blaze with the highest flames. But ultimately a different scheme was chosen. Along with fire-lust, people were hungry. And Ned's second cousin had just spent two years on the dairies of Waikato in New Zealand, where he had picked up the art of cooking meat by burying it underground. This was what they would do, he was shouting. Waving a shovel with one hand, spilling beer with the other.

Ned was fresh from the drive. Stiff and sober, unlike the other men around him, who were all drinking fast and energetically. He watched them, his first bottle cooling his grip, as they began following the directions his second cousin was yelling out. Four of them found shovels and began hacking at the grass, ripping up black loam, carving out a rectangle roughly the size of a child's coffin. A few others lurched into a shed and came out with a cutting block, an axe, armfuls of firewood. They took turns slamming the axe head into slabs of green timber, belting off shards of eucalypt. None of the choppers or diggers let the work get in the way of their drinking, which continued at pace, between the dives of shovels, the thud of the axe.

Another group of men marched down to the river, sent for stones that were apparently vital to the cooking process. Ned watched them go. Thought about joining them. Thought about getting to know this dark river a bit better, getting a feel for its sharp elbows, its muddy banks. Then, with no warning, she emerged from the crowd of drinkers. Came towards him.

The last time he'd seen her she'd been sunbaking at the cove, the day he'd encountered the leatherjacket, shortly before he'd left for the mainland. He'd carried that day with him all over the farms of the interior, summoning the coolness of the sea as he rode through clouds of hot dust, imagining the touch of the current as he'd bathed in outdoor, dirt-rimmed tubs. Closest of all he'd carried the image of her lying on the rocks under the high sun, wet swimsuit glued to her skin. Gripped the memory like a twisting fish.

Now she wore a blue cotton shirt and stiff work trousers, and had arrived at his shoulder. Looking over at the choppers, the diggers.

'Not going to join in?'

Ned kept himself still. Saw how the men with shovels were flinging upturned dirt at each other. How the axemen had swapped timber for empty beers and were demonstrating the brittleness of the glass, seeing how violently they could shatter each bottle. Brown fragments exploding into their shins.

'Looks like they've got things under control.'

He glanced at her. Couldn't stop himself, had to know if she'd found humour in his dryness. Was worried that he sounded arrogant. But he saw an angle to her lips, a crease to her cheeks. Brown-blond hair curtaining her sharp face. Relief fell through him.

She sipped her drink. 'When'd you get back?'

'Few days ago.'

Then a friend was pulling her by the elbow, needing to talk to her, and she was gone, sucked into a group of people Ned was trying to place from his childhood. As she went, he felt the pull of her. The hooks in him. He gazed at the grass at his feet, then at the black wall of cliffs rising in the distance, cutting into the clouds.

When the pit was dug, a fire was built in its centre. Twigs and kindling were placed into the flames, then the chunks of green eucalypt that had been hacked apart by the choppers. The stones gathered from the riverbank were tossed into the embers, with more logs placed over them so that coals would form and cover every piece of rock. The fire burned down, was built up, burned down, built up. Red-winking coals accumulated. A truckload of other men swerved into the paddock, fresh crates of beer sliding in the tray of the vehicle.

Through all this Ned felt the hooks catch, yank, tear. Spent gallons of energy avoiding the urge to look for her, watch her. The effort drained him; he couldn't follow what people were saying to him, couldn't concentrate on the details of people's lives, what they'd done while he was on the mainland. Nothing stuck in him; every conversation passed through him, insubstantial as smoke. He wished Jackbird was there to do the work of talking.

After an hour or so the rocks had reached a temperature his second cousin was happy with. He began shouting more instructions, pointing and gesticulating. The men lurched into action. With metal-pronged rakes they dragged the ashes and coals and rocks from the pit. None of what was happening made sense to Ned. He squinted at the smoking pit, the smoking rocks.

'Still not going to lend a hand?' She had approached him from the side; he hadn't seen her coming. There was an edge to her voice. An inscrutable scrunch to her face. Ned felt tested, unaware of what the test was. Felt her eyes on him, waiting. He twisted a heel. Shook his head.

'Why not?'

He was about to say something about the state of the other men, the hazards of fire and booze, but stopped himself, realising that they might be her friends or family. All he could manage was: 'I don't want to.'

She kept studying him. Cocked her head, crossed her arms. Her eyes nailing into him. 'What *do* you want?'

When he couldn't answer she glanced at the fire pit, announced that the food would take hours, that she was hungry, that she wasn't going to wait around all night for dinner. She left with a group of other young women, not saying goodbye to him, to anyone.

She was right—the food did take a long time. First the smoking rocks were tipped back into the pit. Then Ned's second cousin emerged from the house with a lamb shoulder, a pork shoulder, a pile of beef ribs. He wrapped them in hessian and placed them on the rocks, then covered the hole with a large sheet that had been dragged through the river. Heavy sacks were placed over this sheet, and soil was kicked over the sacks, sealing the heat in. For five hours the meat steamed underground, five hours of further drinking, carousing, occasional resting. At one point some men began throwing hay bales at each other. Someone tried to chop down one of the lone gums and snapped his axe handle in half, and was lucky the splintered end didn't blind him as it rebounded. By the time the food was ready it was dark. Dirt and cloth were dragged off the pit, and they slipped the tender meat off hot bones beside spot fires burning through thick grass meant for dairy cows.

The whole time Ned sipped slowly at his beer, untethered from the revelry around him. Still feeling the heat of her gaze on his face. Replaying their encounter, the boldness in her voice. Wondering if he'd disappointed her. Wondering what he wanted.

A week later he knocked on her father's door and asked if he could come calling for tea at a later date. She pushed into the hallway, asking what was wrong with right now. The same look on her face: the same bold test. Half a year later, they married. It never felt to Ned like a decision he made consciously. It just came up to him, palmed his shoulder, pulled his wrist.

~

Three days after their wedding they were standing at the base of Liffey Falls, at the brisk death of winter, watching an airborne river thrash its way earthward. The water tumbled through high ridges, crowded with the princes of the island's wetter wildernesses: blackheart sassafras, dappled leatherwoods, contortions of mossy myrtles. Giant stringybarks rose above them all, their gum-topped crowns fighting for space in the clouds. The forest loomed, wet-dark and thickly green in the morning dew, and through the ancient roots of its trees the Liffey ran and broke and fell to splash the boots of the gazing newlyweds.

Ned felt her shiver against his arm, and at the shaking of her flesh he began to remove his coat. She had softened during the courtship, peeling off layers of sternness the closer they came to each other. He was still getting used to the touch of her. The nearness of her. They'd spent the previous night in the highlands, in another second cousin's cabin on a fog-drenched sheep farm. The night before that had been their first together, but as it had come at the end of the wedding day, a day of meandering speeches and frenzied dancing and countless toasts, they'd collapsed into the sheets exhausted, drunk, untouching. So it wasn't until that second night, on the sheep farm high on the rocks of the island's roof, that they removed each other's clothes.

Ned had slept with women during his year as a rouseabout's picker-upper, after evenings spent in the grand country pubs of the interior. Often they were older women who'd liked his lack of words, his smile. But these encounters were always rushed, mechanical, awkward. Always he'd woken alone. And when he recalled them, even the most stirring of these memories were dulled by the vats of beer he'd drunk beforehand.

He'd never known the touch of sober skin. Hadn't known the slowness of it. The gentleness, the rhythm. That the pleasure of it all ran far past the pure physicality and into the hours afterwards, those hours of talk and non-talk and blanket-wrapped closeness. In the lanolin-tainted air of the highland cabin he'd felt the heat of her breath on his shoulder, felt the tick of the pulse in her wrist through the flesh of his chest. Remembered her on the dairy farm, asking what he wanted. Felt a swelling expansion within the shadowed corners of himself. He wondered at the course his life had taken and was taking. Couldn't recognise himself in the high darkness. All sorts of things seemed possible; all kinds of evolutions and journeys lay open, their paths raked clear, their stones washed in blinding light.

In the morning they'd felt for each other and found a way to break the frame of his cousin's bed. He had wanted to fix it; she had laughed and made him leave a note declaring they'd found it that way. Afterwards he'd driven them across the plateau, through white-fingered fog, through ghostly stands of cider gums, through thick-needled pencil pines, through plains of buttongrass and tarns, through old rock and fresh lichen, until the road twisted and dived into a golden valley. Here, at winter's end, thousands of wattles had unfurled their gaudy colours. As they descended from the heights their vision was swarmed by the yellow fuzz. Every slope, every scree, every patch of forest, every glimpse through every window was a scene of flowering gold.

The forest's garish decorations were too much. Ned was still woozy at the closeness of the night, at the splintering of the morning. She pointed at the wattles, gripped his knee. He blinked at the bushy goldness. A sluggish buzzing started up beneath his skin. Somehow he piloted them down the muddy road. Somehow he got them to the car park; somehow he followed her past the trees and ferns and torrenting Liffey to the base of the falls. His steps fell slowly, strangely. He had never been so aware of another person's body.

So when the river's spray hit her skin and he felt her shake, he moved to keep that body safe. He pulled off his coat. And as he draped it over her shoulders, the memory was triggered. The other coat, the one he'd shivered into on that star-heavy night. The boat. The mad whale. His father, his brothers. The stillness of the estuary, so much bigger than the tumbling Liffey.

He saw his wife wade into the too-big sleeves of his coat, saw the wool envelop her frame, and the warm jolt that the sight zapped through made him remember: Toby had loved him. Had made that love clear, even if it was always wrapped in jokes and banter. Maybe Toby had been the one to lend him the coat that night on the boat, as they waited for the whale. Bill probably hadn't even realised Ned was there. But under the stark light of the stars, Toby could have seen how Ned shivered, felt sorry for the little brother he loved and tossed his coat across the planks. Thinking of the scene this way made it seem possible, even likely. Ned tried to put his mind back in the boat, tried to remember that moment before the mad whale struck, tried to recall which direction the coat had come from.

As always, he saw only the night-dark river. Felt only the rip of his fear.

# 9

THE LETTER FROM Murmansk tied a knot within Maggie. In the days after its arrival she began shifting about the orchard in looser, slower movements. She spent more time in the sun. She lost interest in the chicken coop. She tinkered with the garden beds, then dragged a pitchfork through them. She stopped staying up to talk with their father in the evenings.

When Ned told her about the mare, she did not congratulate or thank him. She only wiped at her forehead and squinted at the window. 'So she'll live?'

'She should.'

Still Maggie seemed unmoved. Ned's hands found his pockets. He waited for her to realise the value of what he'd done, the independence and ingenuity of it. But she only asked if he was waiting for a medal and, before he could answer, left him in the house and moved out into the summer light.

Ned felt all kinds of heat, all shades of shame. He saw the limping mare as he'd led it through the dawn. Saw the wet stone flying from its hoof. He opened his mouth to call after Maggie, but nothing came out. His fingers tore at the fabric of his shorts.

He was confident he'd get a better reaction from his father, whom he told later that morning, before the day had raked the old man's mind apart. They were out in the orchard, checking for blight and rot. When Ned finished talking, it was a while before his father spoke. Eventually he asked Ned if he knew how much a vet costs.

'I've fixed it.'

'Not your horse. Not your bill to pay.'

'Gonna trap rabbits for the vet. She's got a rabbit problem.'

'Does she.'

'They're destroying her garden.'

His father's face began to fracture; furrows dug around his eyes, a twitch played at his mouth. 'Could have sold it. Lot of things you can do with a lame horse. Plenty of fellas with clever ideas. Plenty of them keen to buy a knackered mare.'

Ned felt the morning swirl. 'I didn't know.'

His father clicked his tongue. 'The things you don't know.' He looked away from Ned. Large breaths moved through his chest.

They continued working, and did not speak for the rest of the day.

After dinner Ned went to a bend in the river where he'd once seen a group of ducks. There he combed through the reeds, under rocks, between roots and in the prickling bracken, hoping to find a nest. He knew little of their laying habits, but he didn't imagine that duck eggs would be too hard to find.

The evening was warm. The work involved a lot of crouching. After an hour he'd found no eggs, and this failure gave him an excuse to become furious, to give in to all the things that were biting and burning at him. He spat and shook. He swore. He slipped on wet clay, he wept, he threw a rock at a sprinting native hen. He wanted to scream. He did not have the language to express the sharpness of what he was feeling. Later, he dropped some dried rabbit into the quoll's crate, not checking on its condition.

~

But then there was the forest behind the vet's place: a forest of tall ferns and bright fungus, of steady soil and thick-trunked trees, of clear streams and cool shade, of unknowable, intricate depths. A place of dark-eyed wallabies and fat-faced possums and flickering wrens and eagle-sized ravens and swarms of rabbits beyond counting, beyond thought. A place so thoroughly non-paddock and non-river and non-orchard that, when he picked his way through its structures, Ned began to unmoor from the leafy dirt and drift away from the version of the world he knew. A wave of prickles needled through him. He felt a shifting beneath his flesh: all his pain and shame and anger and sorrow would peel off his nerves, steam from his bones and fry off his skin.

He was getting up earlier now, before the sun rose, while the ground was cool and the paddocks dark, before Maggie was awake, before even his father was knocking about the kitchen. He'd strap his rifle to his back, fill his pockets with bullets and ride his bike to the vet's, bumping over the corrugations in the gravel. He'd reach the property before the light did. At dawn he was checking the traps he'd set the day before. By the time the sun had fully risen, his hands were full of death.

It seemed to Ned that these forest rabbits were in a rush to escape the summer. Each morning he'd find at least two of their corpses in the teeth of his traps, sometimes three. He'd skin them at the edge of the garden and hurl the bodies far into the trees.

After he'd stashed the skins in his bag he'd move through the forest, towards the small clearings that lay within its interior. Here other rabbits inched over the grass, grazing at pace, their cheeks swelling in the low light. Ned stepped quietly, made sure he was obscured by the darkness of the ferns, waited. He'd raise the rifle and pick out the fattest animal, the cleanest fur. Missing was difficult, although occasionally he managed it.

The clearings would yield an extra three or four rabbits. When the last of them had blinked into the bush he began making his way back, no longer bothering to land his feet quietly. It was in this part of the day, his bag heavy with pelts, his body shaded by blue gum and silver banksia, that he felt the unmooring, the needling, the shifting. The burning away of his emotions, until he saw only the forest around him, and felt only the weight of his bag and gun, and the warmth of the morning.

Back at the garden, he'd find the vet drinking tea on a bench by a rosemary bush. He'd shake the skins at her. She'd raise her mug. In the trees, ravens picked apart his kills.

~

Outside of those mornings in the forest he was exposed to an uncontrollable stinging in the folds of his mind, of the same kind he'd felt while searching for duck eggs. To counter this, he avoided thinking about anything that brought on the sting. The war. The school year that awaited him. The mare. The quoll. Maggie, ice hammered from metal ships, northern seas of endless chop. The rush of Toby's smile, and how soon they might see each other. His father. How his father, after he'd read Toby's letter, had asked Ned if anything had come from Bill. The blank fissure in the old man's face when Ned had shaken his head.

He wrestled all of this from his mind, and replaced it with dreams of trapping, of hunting and, most frequently, of the boat that was drifting closer to him with each fur-smeared trap, each blood-wetted bullet.

Sometimes Bill—tall, soundless, inscrutable—crashed past these visions of the boat. He wouldn't let Ned's thoughts remain on the surface of the water, so Ned would dive beneath it. He'd run to the river and return to its floor, thrashing through the current's nag, thorns in his eyes, choke in his neck, ugly strokes pulling him to the dark sand, to coldness and cleanness.

~

Later in the week he saw more ravens, this time on the edge of a clearing. He was taking aim when his eyes were drawn upwards to jagged flashes in the sky. Three of them were harassing a white goshawk, mobbing it as it arced through the blue. The combat appeared both vague and choreographed; the ravens flapped, darted, stabbed, while the hawk evaded each attack at what seemed like the last possible moment, gliding away from its glossy assailants without seeming to pay them much attention. Their shapes, their ferocity, their movements: it brought to mind the battles Ned had read about at school. Hoplites wrapped in leather and bronze, jamming spears into the spokes of chariots. Muddy knights hauling maces through fog at tinny helmets. Cavalry officers pulled from their mounts by vengeful sepoys. Sailors blasted off rigging, thumping onto softwood decks. Redcoats spilling powder. Bayonets thrusting up from trenches. Slouch hats shot from sweating scalps.

On the way home, with this violence still in him, he crossed through Jackbird's property. The day was clear. Other birds now wheeled through the cloudless sky: black cockatoos, seagulls, swamp harriers.

It did not take him long to find her.

Callie held the shotgun low as she watched a hawk circle a far paddock. It was smaller than the goshawk Ned had seen that morning, smaller too than a swamp harrier. Some kind of falcon or sparrowhawk. Callie didn't seem interested in shooting at it.

When she saw him, Ned came to a stop. 'Seen any duck eggs lately?'

She shook her head. 'Plenty of chicken eggs. What do you want duck eggs for?'

'Vet says that's what I should feed the quoll.'

Colour came to her face. 'It's still alive?'

'Yep.'

'And you've still got it in that crate.'

'I do.'

Callie tilted her neck. 'Duck eggs.'

'What she told me.'

'Ducks down by the river.'

'I know that. Can't find any eggs, though. Thought you might know how.'

She looked to the water, shook her head. 'Don't know the first thing about ducks. My brother does. He brings eggs back for Mum sometimes. Should ask him.' She looked back at Ned. 'Why didn't you?'

Ned shifted his weight. 'Nobody else knows about it. Want it to remain that way.'

'You gonna keep it?' The brightness returned to her cheeks.

'No.' He faltered. 'Don't know.'

~

He found Jackbird at the jetty, smacking a sinker against the riverbed, scaring away any flathead that might otherwise have considered taking the clump of bluebait he'd mashed onto his hook. He was thrilled to see Ned, thrilled to have someone to talk to, something to do other than not catch fish. When Ned asked him about ducks he couldn't reel his line in fast enough. He took Ned to the shoreline, waving an arm, slipping over tide-licked rocks.

'You gotta think like a duck. Act like a duck. No more old steady-Neddy. Where would a duck hide her eggs from water rats and native cats? In the reeds, mate. Under bushes. Nooks, crannies, foliage. It's all about shade and foliage. My cousin taught me. He sells them at the market. Quack, quack, don't let 'em crack. See? Here.'

His hand was under a tree root. It came out holding a blue-white egg, flecked with mud. Jackbird held it up to Ned's eye.

'The brain of a waterfowl is a curious thing.'

Throughout the rest of the afternoon they found four eggs, all in different places. Ned could see no commonality in the locations—cutting grass, beneath rocks, in patches of dead bracken—but Jackbird had a nose for them, could discern a pattern Ned could not. He seemed to think Ned was gathering them for Maggie, and talked incessantly about poached duck eggs, scrambled duck eggs, duck-egg custard, duck-egg scones, duck-egg tart. Ned nodded along. He felt queasy at the deception, but did not correct Jackbird's assumptions.

When the sun dipped, Ned thanked him and took the haul back to the quoll. It still couldn't rise, but its eyes were sharp, and at the sight of Ned it gaped its jaws in a wide yawn before snapping at his hand. He dropped an egg onto the straw. The quoll sniffed at it. Twitched its whiskers. Grabbed the egg with its front paws, lifted it to its snout and cracked it open with a hard bite. It plunged its nose into the opened egg and licked at the contents with energetic hunger. When it was finished Ned dropped in the other three, which it devoured even faster. As it ate, its wounded leg remained still, stretched out in the crate at a stiff angle. Fragments of brittle shell clung to its face fur. Yolk clotted the pinkness of its nose.

~

There seemed no end to the rabbits, no matter how many he harvested from the forest. Soon he began running out of rafters to hang their skins from. The summer burned on. Blood and sunshine filled his days.

At this time of year the heat could turn and ruin a pelt in hours. He could no longer wait for Jackbird's father to take him to Beaconsfield, so he began filling a sack with skins and cycling into the town. Old Singline came to expect him; haggling became a formality; money piled in the dust beneath his bed. It was thorough work: rising early, riding to the vet's, trapping and shooting and skinning, riding home, working in the trees, checking fruit, riding to town, riding home, fossicking for eggs, feeding the quoll, trying to be useful to Maggie around the house and yard. It left his eyes red, his body sore. He liked these days—liked how they hollowed him out.

When he was drained like this he took care to hold on to his secrets, to not reveal the quoll's existence to Maggie or his father, or let his boat fervour slip out his mouth. But even in his exhaustion, keeping the secrets wasn't hard. Maggie was still remote and muted, and didn't ask him much. And he was seeing less of his father. The old man was rarely in the orchard when Ned returned from the vet's, or near the shed, or in the house. Occasionally Ned spotted him in a far paddock, closer to the river, but otherwise he had no idea where the old man was going. He didn't try to find out. He figured his father was still upset with him for the business with the mare, and Ned thought it best to stay out of his way. Usually he only saw him at dinner. All Ned had to do was chew his potatoes and stay quiet.

Some afternoons Jackbird joined him in the search for duck eggs, and Ned began to see what his friend was looking for: the foliaged dents and shadowed gullies that would suit a duck's intentions. Muddy shells began revealing themselves to him. If they found no eggs, they'd swim. Other days—sometimes the same day—Callie would appear on the property without her brother. One morning Ned found that she'd let herself in and removed the crate's lid to stare at the quoll. He wanted to tell her to stay away. Found that he couldn't.

The quoll was recovering well. It could now limp around the crate as its bandaged leg began to unstiffen. Its appetite was strong, for both eggs and rabbit meat, and it showed no signs of pain when he handled it before and after cleaning the crate. Its gums were pink, its teeth white and clean. But most notable was the change to its coat, which had dulled and matted after the injury. Now it was returning to the condition it had been in when he'd trapped it. All the blemishes were gone, either through natural recovery or through the quoll's increased grooming. Straight, strong hairs covered it from snout to claw. Vigorous colour shone in the oak-wood fur, the stark white spots.

# 10

NORTHWEST OF THE river mouth there was a jagged reef. It was well known, well marked, well understood. Yet shipmasters still found its teeth.

The wrecks had been occurring ever since colonial craft began nosing their way into the river, twelve and a half decades before Ned was born. In that time many ships had been caught on the reef and subsequently torn apart as waves hammered them against the rocks. Smaller boats had been lost too: ketches, schooners, dinghies.

Ned had been hearing about them his whole life. The reasons recorded were varied: rough weather, inattention, misunderstanding the flags raised at the pilot station, drunkenness, infighting, poor reading of the tides, sabotage, rocks that reared from waves like snapping hydra-mouths. Each excuse could be understood individually; collectively, the mass destruction made little sense. Locals came to expect carnage whenever they saw sails. Orchardists like Ned's father wouldn't venture past the heads.

As Ned came closer to owning a boat—or so he believed—the stories of these wrecks began floating into his river dreams. The ships killed by the reef began sailing alongside him in his fantasies, holes gaping in their hulls, loose cargo and grey-bodied sailors bobbing in their wake. He'd try to focus on the simple pleasures behind his ambition: the wind whipping the salt off his nose, the freedom of the river's course, the hidden places he would discover, his brothers' expressions when they saw him out on the water.

And in the mornings, as his dreams ebbed away, the boat thirst was still thick in his blood.

~

He was returning from the vet's one morning when he heard the rumble of an engine on the road behind him. Ned pulled his bicycle to the side of the gravel to give the truck room, but instead of rolling past, it came to a stop. A window cranked down. Jackbird's grin leaned out. 'Need a lift? We're going to town.'

He opened his door, slid across the bench seat. Ned hesitated.

Jackbird whacked at the cushion. 'Come on. What else you gonna do today?'

Jackbird's father leaned over from the driver's seat. 'Throw your bike in the back. We can stop at your place to get the rest of them, if you need to.' He pointed at the furs overflowing from Ned's bag.

Ned wavered. Going would reveal his skins to Jackbird, but it would save at least two long rides into town—a day's worth of hunting. He tossed his bike on the tray and climbed into the cab.

Jackbird immediately started going through Ned's bag, fingers flicking over the stacked pelts. Ned made his face flat, looked straight ahead. When they stopped at Limberlost he got out, ran to the shed, collected his other pelts and returned. At the sight of these extra furs, bundled high in Ned's arms, Jackbird could no longer hold back.

'What'd a rabbit ever do to you?'

His father threw a hand at the base of Jackbird's skull, steered onto the road, kept his eyes straight. 'That's nothing compared to what he's sold already. Ned's been busy, son.' Jackbird grabbed at the part of his head his father's hand had collected. 'I live in hope that his work ethic will rub off on you.'

In town they agreed to meet Jackbird's father back at the truck an hour later. The boys walked off, Jackbird babbling questions, Ned giving vague and short answers. He felt control ebbing away, didn't know how to regain it. At Singline's he told Jackbird to stay quiet. For once, Jackbird stopped talking.

The deal went quickly: an inspection of pelts, a brief discussion of money, a fast agreement. Singline pushed the money over his bench, Ned stacked the skins in a dark corner out of the sun's reach. He was aware of Jackbird's restlessness at his back. When they returned to the street, his friend was vibrating.

'How much have you made?'

'A bit.'

'Heaps, then.'

'I didn't say that.'

'And you weren't gonna tell me?'

'What's to tell? Been trapping and shooting. Figured you were doing the same.'

'What're you gonna do with the money?'

'Not certain I'll do anything.'

'Bullshit.' Jackbird started walking, kicking stones, reeling off his thoughts. 'You could get a new reel. New hooks, new sinkers. Better line. We'll actually catch something. Or a new bike, maybe. You need one. The chain's about to rust off the thing you're riding at the moment. You need new boots too. Sorry, mate, but you do. You need new everything. Or how about a new rifle? One with a scope. Hit starlings on the wing. You could...'

'I was thinking a boat.' The words came out unbidden. He couldn't help it.

Jackbird stopped. His eyes shot wide. 'Oh, Neddy.' A breath paused in his chest. 'Yes.'

He ran across the street. Ned called after him, had no choice but to follow. He was angry, swearing, more at himself than Jackbird. At how he'd let his plan unravel. How little control he had over himself.

Ned caught up to him beside a wire fence. Beyond it lay two rows of raised yachts, keels plunging dirtward, masts towering into the sky. Behind them were a group of scattered dinghies. Ned turned to Jackbird. 'No.'

'We've got time.' Jackbird was already walking through the gate.

Ned thought about staying outside but realised how petulant that would look, so he followed him in. Nobody else was in the boatyard. Just dry yachts, dry boats, dry earth. A tall white gum leaned in a corner, bark hanging in curled strips from its pale trunk.

Once Ned was in the yard, surrounded by sleek metal and smooth timber, his buzzing worries settled. A quiet thrill rattled through him. Jackbird darted around the yachts, bending his neck, whistling at their size, but Ned moved straight to the dinghies. There was a range of sizes, of designs, some with simple bench seats, others with semi-enclosed cabins. All were clean and seemed in good condition. Fresh paintwork coated each wooden slat, each miniature detail. The colours glowed in the sunlight. Red, blue, white. Ned wondered if the owner of the boatyard was French.

These dinghies were gorgeous things. He tugged his mind, put himself in each boat, put the boats on the river. Tried to imagine tacking into a wind. How each would handle the swirl of currents off Limberlost's shore. He put a hand to a stern. Imagined water drenching his calves as he pushed out into the water. Saw himself leap into the hull.

'So that's where your money's headed.'

Jackbird's father. He was standing behind Ned, arms crossed. Ned snapped up straight and felt an instinct to apologise. Jackbird's father leaned around him.

'Not many people buying boats right now. You'd get a good price, I imagine. But you can't have enough for one of these.'

He was looking at the little wooden sign at the base of the closest dinghy's frame, the sign Ned had seen and tried to ignore. The number—like the numbers on all the other signs like it—was higher than he'd expected. Far higher than anything he could afford, even if he doubled his output, if he purged every rabbit from the valley.

'No, sir.'

Jackbird's father patted his shoulder. 'Worth looking, I suppose. Although I'm sure you didn't have a new boat in mind.'

Ned nodded, even though it wasn't true. He'd not had any particular boat in mind—just built, second-hand, falling apart. None. He hadn't let his ambitions coalesce into a strategy. He'd just planned on making money, and assumed a boat would follow, as greenness follows rain. Here in the yard, in the company of grand craft and impossible numbers, he felt foolish. A greedy dreamer.

Jackbird kept mooning around the yachts. His father looked at Ned again. Read the trouble in his face. 'Good thing I know a bloke.'

~

On the way home they took a left, barrelling south down a narrow road. Through a grove of tall blue gums, past stony paddocks. A small cliff rose before them, gashes of yellow and white in the rock of its face.

Jackbird's father turned into a barely discernible driveway and drove across dirt until they reached a small house and a set of sheds. Beside the last building sat four dinghies. Ned looked away from them. Looked at anything else: wilted grass, sandy rock, the ochred tin roofs of the sheds.

After pulling up, Ned and Jackbird lingered by the truck, not wanting to spread out over whoever's land it was, as Jackbird's father knocked at the door. It opened. Words were passed. An old man came out, or perhaps he wasn't old: a man greyed and beaten, in patched trousers and dusty boots. His eyes were pinched. The creases in his face were deep, but the skin around them did not sag. He could've been forty-five or seventy. He took the boys in without interest. Jackbird's father beckoned them.

'Lads, this is Mr Falmouth.' He indicated each of the boys. 'This is my son, Jack, and this is William West's youngest, Ned.'

Falmouth kept looking at them. Stiff hair matted his scalp and fuzzed over his chin. Ned wondered if something within the man was broken or jarred. He was a loose sketch—unfinished, or in parts smudged out.

Jackbird's father continued. 'Ned here is in the market for a piece of watercraft. Nothing fancy. Thought he might be able to take one off your hands. Isn't that right, Ned?'

Ned felt Falmouth's eyes settle on him. Wanted to shrug, wanted to say no, or maybe, or that he wasn't sure.

'Yes, Mr Falmouth.'

Falmouth grunted. He began walking to the dinghies. Ned followed, Jackbird poking at his ribs. Falmouth stopped at the closest boat. 'They're all for sale.'

His voice was a wiry scratch. Ned began to look at the dinghies properly, without knowing what he was looking for. They were all lying on the bare dirt, in various states of disrepair. Falmouth was staring as well. Dull revelation on his face, as if he was seeing them for the first time.

'Were my son's. He wanted to fix 'em up. He won't be coming back from the Pacific, so that plan's done.' Falmouth blinked at the boats. 'The boy had funny ideas...I don't know. Not funny.'

Ned found that when Falmouth said these things he

couldn't look him in the face. He shifted away, focused on the boats. As a collection, they did not look like much. Four beaten-up old tubs, sure to be leaky, sure to be treacherous. The smallest would barely hold two adults, while the largest, with its long sweep oar, looked like a retired surfboat. All wore rough wounds in their woodwork. Many of these markings went beyond superficial damage: planks were bent and warped, light worked its way through splintered gaps.

One had a mast, although it wasn't up; it lay flat in the hull, unattached to the centreboard. It was to this boat that Ned was drawn. A mast meant a sail, which Ned thought important, although there was no sail to be seen. The boat was a drab olive colour. Long scratches ran through its faded paintwork. One of the oars stashed within its body was snapped off halfway down the handle. The bench seat was broken. There was a notch for a rudder, but no rudder in sight. Yet it was not structurally damaged, at least to Ned's eye, nor did it have any of the gaping holes that the other dinghies did. And the timber revealed by the peeled-back paint was not grey or brown but a hazy, curious blond.

Jackbird noticed Ned's attention. He kicked a boot into its side, rocking it nearly over, sending dust flying.

'Looks like it's in one piece,' he said.

Ned turned to Falmouth. 'How much?'

The man did not appear to think much of the question. He took a flap of the paint and tore it free. It crumbled in his fingers, leaving an oily smear and flecks of green on his skin. More blond wood appeared where the paint had been, almost bright, almost shining. Falmouth named a price.

The boat was worn, damaged. Perhaps beyond repair. It was missing vital parts.

Ned nodded. 'I have to check a few things first.' Hard fingers gripped his lungs.

~

On the drive home Jackbird saturated the truck with his thoughts on what they should do with the boat. Fishing, sailing, exploring—the things Ned had already obsessed over all summer. But Jackbird's ideas did not end where Ned's did: they included setting drumlines for sharks, boarding other vessels, lassoing and enslaving dolphins in an effort to turn the boat into a kind of ocean chariot, shooting albatrosses, and convincing the daughters of the rich cattle farmers on the eastern side of the river to sail with them all the way to Flinders Island.

In this wash of talk Ned remembered that Jackbird hadn't gone to the river mouth during the reign of the mad whale. Had only ever known a flat river.

It was only when his father commented that Ned would be the owner, not both of them, and that a lot of work needed to be done in order to get it seaworthy, that Jackbird relented. He turned his words to asking Ned when he'd buy it, how he'd fix it, where he'd store it. Ned said little in response.

They arrived at Limberlost in the late afternoon. Once he'd thanked Jackbird's father and said goodbye, Ned did not go into the house or shed. He walked to the orchard. He walked past each row of trees, scanned each leafy corridor. The harvest was still over a month away, but already the fruit was red and swollen. Branches dipped with the weight of their crop.

After finding nobody in the apple trees Ned moved to

the empty paddocks. He crested the two small hills at the back of the property. He threaded through the old black gums the family had reserved for firewood. He looked over to the road, to the driveway, back to the shed. He considered the ground he hadn't covered. He thought of going back to the house, helping Maggie, checking on the quoll, running a peeler over some potatoes. But he kept walking, eventually reaching the waterline, where he finally found his father, pushing a wheelbarrow overburdened with planks of wood towards the northern boundary of the property.

When his father saw him, he set the legs of the wheelbarrow down. Adjusted his hat, waited for his son to start speaking. Ned could see how the old man was reading the nervousness in him. Felt pinned, exposed.

Eventually he found his words. 'You know how I've been selling those rabbit pelts.'

'I'm aware.'

'Well, I've been saving the money.'

'Good lad.'

'I've saved quite a lot.' Ned waited for his father to respond. He didn't, so Ned swallowed, stiffened. Paused. 'I thought I might buy a small boat.'

Once he'd said it, Ned felt light-headed. His father was watching him with an unfathomable expression. Ned couldn't tell if he was angry, astonished, happy or disgusted. His hat was shadowing his face, which made it even harder for Ned to read him.

His father picked up the wheelbarrow. 'Come with me.'

He rolled forward over a faint path in the grass. Ned

followed him. Kept holding on to his words, his explanations and excuses. He waited for his father to tell him that he'd thought Ned was raising money for the war, for hats like the ones his brothers had been issued, that they didn't need a boat, that it would only cost them more money in upkeep, that didn't Ned realise the position they were in, hadn't he heard his father and Maggie talking in the evenings, that a boat was a luxury they didn't need or deserve, that his thoughtlessness was only surpassed by his selfishness. But he said nothing. Ned decided this silence was part of his punishment. Or that his father couldn't shape words around his disappointment.

Ned was watching his feet fall, his thoughts torn, on fire, when his father stopped. Ned nearly walked into him. They were near the water, in the crook of one of the river's elbows. A small pebbly beach ran along the shore. At its back, near a stand of peeling paperbarks, had appeared a small shed.

Ned moved to its doorless entryway. Saw the old, reused planks that formed its walls and its rough raised floor. The uneven rafters, not yet sheathed in roof slats. Its existence shook the teeth in his gums. Shook the thoughts from his head.

His father came to his side. 'We'll need to finish the roofing, lay some runners on the beach.'

Ned turned. His voice was unsteady. 'How long have you known?'

'Since I spoke to Telle, the day after you took the horse down to her.'

Ned searched his mind until he remembered the name: Estelle. The vet. Jackbird's father had said it once. Ned laid a hand on the shed's wall. 'How long have you been building it?'

'Since around then.'

'I was going to tell you.'

'And now you are.'

Ned saw how the inscrutability had fallen from his father's face: saw the hint of a smile curling his mouth. The spark of pleasure in his creek-clear eyes.

'You're a funny fella. Nothing wrong with working towards a goal. One of the better things a man can do. Long as you earn what you're after.'

'I was doing it to help make hats as well.' Ned heard the earnestness in his voice, the high strain of justification. 'The pelts will make good hats. You said so yourself.'

His father grabbed a plank from the wheelbarrow, held it up to the roof. Measured with his eye. 'I don't give two bob about slouch hats.' He lowered the plank, laid it against the shed's wall and began stacking the others beside it. 'This boat. Can you afford it?'

'Yes.'

'And have you any idea how to sail it?'

'Some.'

'How much?'

'Not much.'

'Well.' He indicated the shed with a dip of his neck. 'At least it'll be safe when it's out of the water.'

Ned swallowed. 'Thanks.' Knew he should say more, but could get no more words out. Nothing in his short, tight life had prepared him to convey the amount of gratitude he felt.

His father grabbed another plank. 'Don't expect a birthday present.'

They unloaded the rest of the planks from the wheel-barrow. When they were finished, Ned's father straightened up and looked out at the water. The sun was dying at their backs, shedding long light over weak ripples. The satisfaction disappeared from his features. A crumpling came over his face, and suddenly he looked like Falmouth: age-wrecked, hollow. 'Make sure you take your sister out when you've bought it.'

'I will.'

After a moment his father still looked undone, unravelled, his eyes caught on something beneath the water. Ned felt a need to drag him landward. 'What else did the vet say?'

His father slid his attention from the river, back to Ned. A rough hint of a smile on his face. 'Told me everything. Known Telle since we were kids. Knew her parents.'

Relief poured through Ned. He exhaled, long and slow. 'I thought you'd be mad about the quoll.'

His father's eyebrows dropped. His eyes hardened. His face returned to its usual blankness, its unreadable quietness. 'Quoll?'

# 11

WHEN HE WAS old enough to feel a coarse grating in his knees but still young enough to work outdoors through every hour of daylight, to work without complaint or sourness, Ned went to the saltwater cattle muster in the northwest. He and his wife had recently bought a small orchard, not far from Limberlost. They now had a baby, a girl they'd named Sally. Another child was expected in a few months.

The orchard's fruit was not yet yielding much money, so together with planting more apple trees, they'd put in a large vegetable garden. Ned knew nothing about gardening—all he knew about plants was how to grow apples and fell gums—but his wife had grown up cultivating enough food to supply a small market. She led him through the basics, her old sternness reappearing in the moments he got things wrong, her love winking through afterwards, as they threw loose dirt at each other. They worked hard and although they were sometimes hungry, they were rarely unhappy.

Yet pumpkins and beans would not grow overnight, and Sally was growing, and so was the child in his wife's womb, and they needed money. Mustering wasn't his choice of work but neither, he'd come to realise, was the life of a rouseabout. The work was backbreaking, the sheep were permanently terrified, and the smell of lanolin to Ned was cloying and inescapable. Nor was tree-felling: his time killing the White Knights had left him with a permanent stickiness to his hands and a reddish wound in his soul. Mustering mostly involved sitting on a horse, and it paid well.

Ned had heard about the job from a cousin who wasn't known for exaggerating. He explained it all to his wife. She gave him the look—the bold frankness that still arrested him—and asked what he was waiting for. In the morning he drove northwest.

For the best part of a day he rolled along the coast road, farmland to his left and blue water to his right. Orchards were soon replaced by the churned red soil of potato paddocks. As the world became greener these spud paddocks gave way to vast pastures of grass, used for dairy and beef farming. Ned wondered at the reliable wetness of this place, at rainfall that could be predicted to the fraction of an inch. Where the land was steep he skimmed the remnants of ancient forests. The further he drove, the more prominent these forests became. He knew that if he kept going he would reach the rounded tip of the island and be forced to head south, down the rugged west coast, where the great forests still dominated and the winds were so strong it was rarely possible to get a boat out of harbour. Ned felt a temptation to take this road. To see a white-smashed ocean that stretched all the way to India. To feel the drag of those violent winds.

He pushed on until he found the turn-off, late in the afternoon. It was a coastal property bisected by a river that featured prominent sandbanks and flats near its mouth: the work of a vigorous tide. The river emptied into the same sea that had been on the right of Ned's window all day. Rising from it, a couple of miles from shore, was a flat, green island.

He knew that before this was cattle country it had been sheep country, and before that it had been the hunting grounds of the Pairelehoinner people and the other tribes of the north-west. As he'd grown and worked and moved about, old men had told him this, just as the old people of the valley had once told him about the Letteremairrener. The Pairelehoinner had shaped the land with fire, creating lush tussock-grass plains bordered by white-petalled tea-tree groves—ideal for maintaining populations of wallaby and kangaroo. At some points in the year they would swim across to islands like the one Ned could see now. There they'd hunt island wallabies, as well as gather abalone and shellfish from the shallow straits, mutton-bird chicks from their nests in the dunes. At no point, Ned had heard, were they hungry.

On the farm's edge he found a camp: trucks, swags, cooking fires. Horses were tethered nearby. In the closest paddock, a herd of cows grazed. The men and women in the camp were drinking tea or beer. Ned found the farmer in charge and introduced himself. Mentioned his cousin's name. Mentioned the mainland stations he'd worked on. Didn't mention that he'd been a rouseabout, or more often just a rouseabout's picker-upper, not a jackaroo or stockman. The farmer said only that he'd been expecting him, and that he assumed he could ride.

In the morning Ned was given a horse. By now he was no longer apprehensive of them, or had convinced himself that he wasn't. He still felt the dull ache of the stallion's bite in cold weather, but this morning was warm. He saddled his mount, climbed onto its back and followed the other riders as they moved to the paddock gate.

There the farmer gave them their instructions. They would be taking the herd across the shallows to the rich feeding grounds of the island Ned had seen the day before. For the most part the cattle would be able to walk, although when they crossed the river, and perhaps in other parts, they would have to swim. It was hard to tell exactly where, the farmer said, as the tide regularly tossed the sand about. The riders were to drive the cows forward and ensure they did not turn back or strike out into deeper water.

Ned was directed to the back of the herd and told to watch for stragglers. He didn't know if this was a sign of the farmer's confidence in him—the rear of the herd being the last line of defence—or an indication that he wasn't up to the more difficult task of guiding the herd from its sides. He considered each of these possibilities, before realising he didn't care. He was confident he could handle the work and, as nobody would be watching him, he could sit on his horse and take in the newness of the country they moved through. As long as the cows did not wander he could gaze instead at the shifting sands, the sucking tide and the long stretch of sea-bashed coast, stunning in its rough suit of driftwood, its lonesome shoulders of wind-combed dune grass. The clouds above, like untethered mountains. And before them, drawing his eyes like a lodestar, the rising plain of the island. A green oasis in the ever-chopping ocean.

Getting the cattle out of the paddock, through a path in the dunes and onto the beach was easy work. From there it became tougher. The animals closest to the tideline hesitated; they'd splash about, then stand still or try to turn around. Anguished lowing soaked the air. Eventually, through the urging of the riders and the weight of the bodies behind them, these leading cows were pushed into the waves, and began to drop their hooves into the water. Once they were on their way, it became less difficult to encourage the rest of the herd to follow.

Ned sat his horse on the shore, waiting for the last of the cattle to enter the strait. The wind raced into his face. The estuary before him was a mess of competing currents and varying depths. It looked treacherous, but he told himself that this was not his valley, these were not his waters, that there was every chance it was safe. He couldn't know the personality of this river. When all the cows had waded into it, he took his place behind them and kicked his horse forward.

The herd moved at an uneven pace through the shallows. Some cows seemed unperturbed by the water; others were apprehensive, confused, slow to move. This disparity in speed meant the herd soon became strung out, and its increased length meant the riders patrolling the sides had more ground to cover. As they thrashed back and forth, corralling animals that stumbled off course, Ned was left alone at the rear.

His job, he thought, was easier than that of the side-riders. The cows at the back of the herd seemed more willing to follow the mass of their brethren than to break free from the group. He still had work to do—many of the cattle still needed to be turned in the right direction, or goaded to pick up their pace by a nudge from his horse—but Ned was largely unworried, and quickly became comfortable in his role. He was able to watch this northwest world in the way he'd hoped. To touch its contours, move through its colours.

Soon he began to think of his little orchard, and the scions of golden delicious he'd recently grafted onto the young trees. Hoped the grafts would take. He thought of his wife, his daughter. Felt the buzz of love that comes with a little distance. Let the sea cool his booted feet.

When those cooling waves reached his shins, he was washed back to reality. The cattle had entered the river's centre and begun to swim. The horse could still reach the bottom, but couldn't gallop or even trot at this depth. Up ahead, Ned saw the massed cattle paddling forward, watched by the riders. The cows closest to him followed with increased urgency. Now that they couldn't turn on their hooves, they seemed resigned to following the course set by their herd mates and less likely to break free or try to turn back. Ned relaxed into his saddle and pulled on the reins, giving his horse a rest.

He loosed his mind onto his family again, his hopes for their orchard and future. He didn't notice when a cow turned east and kicked out at a ninety-degree angle, away from the others, until it was a good ten yards off course. When he did, he swore and kicked his mount forward, but by the time he'd come around the back of the other cattle the escapee was well out on its own. Ned surged on. He saw what had caught the cow's eye: a small hump of sand out in the strait, deposited by the tide. The animal had mistaken it for dry land. He plunged his horse into the river, forcing it to swim as well. They managed to circle the cow. Ned kicked out at it. Whistled. Yelled. It seemed to turn around. Ned let out a gasp of relief, steered his horse back to where it could stand. Then the cow doubled back, past Ned, and clambered onto the sandbar.

Ned could hear the deep blowing of his horse's lungs. He let it rest for a moment, even as the rest of the herd receded from them. He looked out at the cow's little island, and saw that the sand wasn't as firm as it looked. The cow's hooves were sinking past its ankles. It kept ripping them free, but every tugged fetlock pushed the remaining three further into the muck.

Ned drew in a breath and tried to harden his body, his mind, as he pushed again into the river's depths. He made straight for the sandbar. The horse did not fight him. After a few tight minutes it found purchase on the island and dragged them both up. The cow blinked at them. Ned immediately brought his horse to its rear, took a crop from his saddle and began pummelling the cow's flank, exhorting it with shouts of abuse and encouragement.

Under this assault, and perhaps at seeing how far it now was from the herd, the cow finally managed to squelch off the sandbar and back into the river. But its energy was sapped. It had spent too much in its escape attempt, and even more in removing itself from the sucking sand. Ned felt it looking at him, exhaustion in its shuddering body. A wet plea in its eyes.

The sea lapped at its mouth and nostrils. Ned circled it again, kicking harder at its side, wailing again with his crop. The cow sprayed water from its nose. It was struggling to keep its head above water.

A shout hit him. An arrhythmic splashing. He looked up and saw a rider approaching. A woman he hadn't spoken to that morning or the previous night, on a tall black horse. She plunged into the depths, yelling something Ned couldn't make out. When she reached him she took a rope from her saddle and threw it over, keeping hold of one end. Ned saw it land by the cow. Understood the rider's plan.

He leaped from his horse and felt the weight of his shirt and boots double, triple, as they took on water. He stroked forward and took the rope in his hands, as his horse swam away from him. The cow was struggling, going nowhere but up and down. He tried to wrap the rope under its stomach, but couldn't reach, and with the burden of his clothes, couldn't dive under it. He splashed forward and clung to the creature's head as he wrapped the rope around its thick neck, aware that he was putting it under further strain. It was becoming harder to swim, harder to stay afloat. He tied off the rope with a prayer that the knot would hold. The cow's nose again went under. He held a thumb in the air.

The cow was yanked forward with ugly strength. Ned let go. Let himself float. After a moment he began paddling back to the shallows, where his horse was waiting for him. A loyalty he felt he did not deserve. He looked to the crossing, and saw that the rider had dragged the cow out of the depths. It was standing on firm sand, shaking and huffing. Ned mounted, rode over. Saw that he'd tied the rope too tight. Saw how it had torn a long, red burn into the cow's neck, from the top of its leg to the base of its head. Parted fur matted on the flesh. Blood oozed from the wound.

The rider looked over at him, a pallid smile on her face. 'Bit of fun.' She turned her horse, kept a hold of the rope. 'We better catch up.'

They took the crossing slowly: the other rider going first, gently pulling on the rope, as Ned and his horse stayed at the cow's back, cajoling it forward. Somehow the animal managed it. On the other side it stumbled, and Ned thought it was going to collapse. But the sound of the herd was in the air, and perhaps a scent of clearer air, of fresh vegetation. The cow found new strength.

Half an hour later they came out of the shallows and onto the beach. They followed the herd's tracks over a path in the scrub, over the yellow dunes, and joined their fellow riders and the cattle on a wide plain of high green grass.

~

Ned knew he was tired, knew his mood was bad. But still he felt cheated. The verdant island he'd imagined was, in reality, a dull disc of pasture. No shady groves of trees, no fresh streams of leaping fish, just an unsheltered paddock. Trees once must have grown here: trees torn from the land by remorseless industry. And when he looked back to where they'd come from, the rest of the coastline had lost its wild character, its romance. Its coarseness was no longer beautiful, but rough and uninviting. He looked for the cow he'd saved, looked for its stripe of opened flesh. Couldn't find it.

After taking a short rest, he and the other stock workers rode back across the river, leaving the herd behind to feed. By the time they reached camp it was nearly dark. Someone got a fire going. A barbecue spat lamb fat. There was beer. Ned inhaled a bottle and looked around for the rider who'd come to his aid earlier. When he couldn't find her, he crawled into his swag.

The next morning he felt like he'd worked four days on a sheep station with no breaks and no water. At the hot breakfast the farmer put on he sipped black tea and marvelled at the weakness of his limbs. A young rider trotted into camp. He'd been sent across to the island at dawn to check on the herd's condition. They were grazing with gusto, he said. All were healthy, except the one that had tried to escape, which had died in the night. The young rider didn't know if it was due to the rope-wound in her neck, or from having swallowed too much seawater, or through sheer exhaustion. Just that she was dead.

After breakfast, the workers packed up their gear and made ready to leave. The farmer walked around the group, handing out envelopes. He came to Ned last. Ned wondered what the price of a cow was, how much would be deducted from his pay. If he'd receive anything at all. He imagined a rope sawing into the soft skin of his flank. The hot cut of its fibres.

The farmer looked him in the eye and handed over the envelope. 'I saw some of what happened. And I spoke to Wendy.' Ned took Wendy to be the rider who'd come to his aid. 'It's happened before, and it'll happen again. There's no teaching these animals. Mind of their own. I don't consider you at fault. And I'm grateful for the effort you put in to saving the damn thing. Lots of men would've let it drown.' He put a hand on Ned's shoulder, then walked on.

As he took the long drive home, Ned told himself to be happy with the pay. It was a good whack of money. But for the whole trip, through forest and pasture and red soil and valley, his mind wouldn't settle. Why couldn't he have turned the cow before it broke free? He thought of Bill sitting tall and alert astride a horse. Of Toby racing fast and hard on another. These memories were old, and brought him throbs of sorrow, yet he could still picture them. How could he have been so careless? Even Jackbird, who had recently taken over his own family's orchard, knew when to pay attention to things. He'd recently found a way to sell apples into Japan. Had done it with a shrewdness that nobody saw coming.

Ned was thirty. When would the natural competence of other men come to him? He knew he had worth. Knew he had qualities that were of value. He knew the farmer had spoken truly: other men would've let the cow drown. But he longed to be more surefooted, for his adult self to be more resolved. To be a person who was complete. He thought of the Pairelehoinner: how they'd hunted the land he was leaving for longer than the empires of Europe had existed. Thought of the wisdom associated with such a thing. He thought of how his father could throw a boatshed together, in secret, easy as ripping off a rabbit's skin.

# 12

'SHOW ME.'

Ned led his father from the boatshed to higher ground. Dread slowed his steps. Behind him the old man was voiceless, heavy-footed. The muted kindness that had pulsed from him at the shore was gone; now all Ned could feel at his back was tight menace. He tried to think of ways he could distract his father, free the quoll. Came up with nothing.

They passed Maggie, hacking at a towering thistle with a hoe. She looked up as they went by. Read something in their quiet march. Ned kept his head down.

Inside the shed he walked to the crate. His father was at his back. Still his mind scrambled for ways out.

'Let's see it.'

Ned hoped the quoll would escape on its own. That when he touched its timber cage it would bunch its legs, and when he removed the lid it would fly up and out, past Ned and his father before they could move, hitting the dirt and sprinting for the gap in the door, its paw strong, its speed impossible.

But when he prised open the crate he found it groggy and docile. A clump of dried yolk hung on its whiskers. Energy left Ned's body, and his dread intensified, pooling in every inch of him. The quoll yawned, showing the bright daggers of its bite. Its coat was glossy, its spots snowy, its footpads pink and firm. At least it was healthy, he thought. At least it had experienced a last flourish of strength.

His father regarded it for a moment before grabbing an old axe handle. Ned felt his pulse craze. His father hefted the tool. Ned wanted to shout, but found that he couldn't. When it noticed Ned's father, the quoll stiffened.

The old man poked the handle into the crate, dangling it as a lure. When the quoll slammed its teeth onto the wood he shot down his free hand and gripped the back of its neck. He raised the quoll to his eye height. It was huge in his grip, bigger than Ned remembered, bigger than a wild cat. Longer than a devil, and nearly equal in weight. It must have grown muscle on its duck-egg diet. It twisted and writhed, turning over and in on itself, its long tail flailing about, but it could not break free or reach its captor's wrist with its snapping teeth. It began to scream. High, coarse barks slammed off the shed's walls. The axe handle hung low.

Ned's guts were plunging, his mouth drying. He wanted to tell his father to look out for its wound, to not disturb the bandage. But his father wasn't there to help the quoll heal. It would only take a single blow. Or maybe, Ned realised, no blow at all. A memory rushed into his mind: Toby talking to him about Bill: *Little twists, a pop, a rip, and the pelt's off. No blade in his hand.* And his father, talking to him only the other week: *Who do you think taught him?*

His father need only flex his hands to remember his old strength. The quoll screamed with the hoarse outrage of a predator undone. Ned hoped it would be quick. That its world would end with the bluntness of speed.

'How'd you catch it?'

It was Maggie. Ned turned and saw her standing in the entryway. His father looked up as well, then indicated his son with an inclined chin. Kept the quoll high.

Ned tried to steady himself. 'Rabbit trap.' Heard the wobble in his voice. 'Near your chicken coop.'

Maggie came forward. 'After I found those marks?'

'Yep.'

She kept coming, past Ned, right up to their father. Buried her face in the quoll's presence. It yowled with fresh fury. Flung claws at her. She leaned back, taking it in. 'Funny type of hawk.'

Ned would have smiled if the muscles in his face weren't so tight. He just wanted his father to do it. To swing the handle, to slam this day shut.

Instead, the old man lifted the quoll higher. Peered at it with a butcher's eye. 'You bunged him up pretty good.' And then he was lowering it, with care, with gentleness, into the crate. The quoll struggled, still trying to rip him apart, but he got it down without catching a wound. On the lid went. Air burst from Ned's lungs.

His father straightened. 'You can't keep it.'

Ned's voice came out half-throttled. 'I wasn't going to.'

'As soon as it can walk, it's gone.' He tossed the axe handle into the shadows. 'I'll say that once.'

'Yes, sir.'

Maggie was on her way out the door. 'A sore paw will be the least of its worries if it comes after my chickens again.'

Ned and his father followed her. They went into the house, took off their boots and damp socks, began doing the things they did at the end of each day: washing their arms and faces, scraping away the grit they'd collected. Ned scrubbed potatoes, boiled water. He was exhausted by the emotions of the day. A month of feeling had been packed into a few bright hours. Usually in these moments of untaxing chores he'd plan and daydream, but his wrung-out mind gave him no ideas to mould, no fantasies to fiddle with. Couldn't think of the shed. Couldn't remember what Falmouth's boat had looked like.

His father disappeared into the other room to pore over the newspaper, staring at the black lines of reports, seeing if he'd missed something when he'd first read them that morning. Reading them again and again and again.

Later at the table, his chewing paused. 'You'd have got good money for that pelt.'

Admonishment or admiration. Ned couldn't tell which.

~

The money dragged at him and he didn't want it anymore; he felt sick at the thought of it under his bed, sick and hot at the idea of it just sitting there. So at dawn he biked to Falmouth's and poured it into the man's palms, who watched the coins land with unshining eyes. They agreed that Falmouth, who owned a truck, would deliver the dinghy to Limberlost later in the week. Ned shook his hand. Felt cold, hard knobs of skin. Tore home on the bicycle, dust clagging the sweat running down his calves.

Jackbird tried to visit, but Ned saw him coming and hid. He didn't want to talk about the boat until it was properly his, didn't even want to think about it. It was too close. He couldn't hold the reality of it straight; the boat blurred his vision, gave him a headache.

He still went to the vet's—Telle, as he'd started thinking of her now—every morning, because rabbits continued to feast on her garden, and his debt had still not been paid. Once he had prised the corpses from the traps around the garden's borders he took to the forest beyond it, as he used to, but no longer with his rifle; he went only as a walker. Felt the settling peace of shade and moss, creek and stone. He wondered if the rest of the world was like this. If forests cooled the blood of people in every type of land and country. If there were places like this in the Pacific. In Murmansk. In Singapore.

Sometimes he thought of the white goshawk. He wondered if it had escaped the ravens. If Callie had blasted it from the sky.

When he saw Telle he asked her why she'd told his father about the boat. She smiled. Soaked the dirt at her feet with dregs of tea.

'Have you tried lying to him?'

Ned pictured the ever-open wound of his father's face.

As he left, Telle told him the mare was nearly healed.

~

There was no warning about the boat's arrival, no ceremony to the occasion. Falmouth and another man who resembled him but without the haunted features, perhaps a brother or cousin, dumped it in the paddock nearest the driveway. Ned saw it

113

happen from the orchard. He watched as they untied the straps holding the dinghy to the flat tray of the truck, then levered it onto the ground. They didn't do it violently, but neither did they approach the task with care. The boat smacked into the soil, rocked on its keel. Looked like it was held together with glue and twine. Ned felt a sheet of regret fall over him. The boat would sink, might even fall apart as soon as he touched it. The moment it hit the dirt Falmouth and his relative got back in the truck and left.

It looked like bad news, there in the afternoon's light, even once it had stopped rocking. It looked worn and dangerous—tired at best. But when Ned approached it, he recognised what had struck him that first time in Falmouth's yard: the clean lines of its shape, the comforting sturdiness, the lager sheen of the wood blinking from beneath the old paint. Hope again edged through him.

In a pile of rusting refuse beside the shed, among tyres and ancient chains and long grass, he found what had once been a cart, or perhaps a small buggy. It was a wreck, but it had two wheels and an axle that remained intact. He rolled it over to the boat, where he lifted the bow onto the axle and secured it with a few lengths of rope. When he raised the stern the whole thing wobbled, and the boat threatened to slide off the buggy. But it was light—far lighter than he'd expected. If he moved slowly he was able to push the contraption forward, and if he dodged the more obvious divots and gullies he was able to keep the boat from shaking free. Down the orchard he rolled, piloting the boat over dry earth. Down to the waterline, through the track his father had made in the bracken, to the half-finished boatshed.

He eased the apparatus into the shed's interior and untied the broken buggy, resting the boat on the boards his father had laid over the sandy dirt. He gave it a long stare. Wondered where to start, what he should do, knowing the whole time that before he got to work on the boat he needed to finish the shed. It was the clear order of things. He wanted to pour himself into the restoration, but he knew it wasn't right to start this new job while another remained unfinished. That was the avenue of the lazy, of malingerers. Of the sort of people his father looked down on.

The old man had made it clear that he was too busy to help out now that the frame was up, that the rest of the job was Ned's. A stepladder was propped against the wall, and beside it lay a pile of planks. Ned knew where others were, up behind the main shed. A jar of nails bristled on the ground.

For two days he worked, following his intuition, not fully knowing what he was doing. Nobody had taught him how to build a shed. He just looked at what his father had already built and imagined a series of steps that needed to be taken next. He hammered planks onto the frame to create a roof. When they didn't fit, or if he hadn't positioned them close enough together, he clawed out the nails with the back of the hammer and started again. He did the same with the walls, doing his best to make sure no light or wind cut between the wood. When small gaps were unavoidable he forced offcuts into the holes, wedging and bludgeoning until a seal was formed.

He knew his workmanship was poor. He knew he was rushing. It was obvious which parts of the shed his father had built, and which were his slapdash contributions. There was a shoddiness to his efforts, an ugliness to the lines of the building, and though he told himself it was rustic charm, he knew that was not true. The eaves were of uneven lengths, the walls leaned at unusual angles. He'd blasted open a thumb while aiming at a nail; his blood had sunk into the timber and dried into splashes of lifeless maroon. But he kept lifting and chiselling and hammering and bleeding until there were no holes in the rafters or walls, until he could throw a bucket of river water over the roof and only a few drops fell through to smack at the shed's interior.

Finally he could turn his attention to the boat. He knew he should paint over it, for practical reasons as well as cosmetic. A proper paint job would protect it from the elements and stop the saltwater from warping it. But he didn't want to captain another bright-splashed, garish thing up and down the river. Picturing that made him twinge, filled his mouth with acid. He wanted something that would not declare itself so loudly. Something that would not crash through the world, but slide into it.

He kept looking at the timber beneath the flakes of the paint. Its colour followed him everywhere. A hazy straw, so unlike hard gum or dark oak. It would need to be treated. It might be of a type unsuitable for saltwater; perhaps that's why it had languished in Falmouth's yard for so long.

Yet the wood kept at him. In it Ned saw gold, saw nature, saw heaven. Wider possibilities seemed within reach in a boat that refused to hide a colour like that. He imagined it melding into the river's morning slate, its blondness playing against the soft notes of dawn. It didn't feel like he made the decision, the wood just insisted, and then he was holding his breath and scrubbing sandpaper down the boat's flanks, tearing paint away in flecks and strips, an olive cloud speckling the air.

~

It took him a single long day to remove the paint. With an old shirt tied around his nose and mouth he attacked the hull, the stern, the bow, the decking, the centreboard, the oars, the space where a rudder would sit. He tore through his first length of sandpaper within an hour and was lucky to find another roll of it in his father's toolbox. By the end of the day more than half of it had been eaten up by the work. His shoulders hurt, his back hurt, his arms hurt. His fingers were clawed up with ache. The floor and walls of the boatshed were smothered in the clinging dust of dead paint. His skin was a mess of green marks, his hair was matted with green drippings, his clothes were a scene of green ruination. Even the light was stained green by the particles in the air.

But beneath that verdant cloud, the boat was free. Ned circled it, appraised it. When he was sure that every smear of paint had been stripped from every plank, he stepped back into the doorway to view the vessel in its naked entirety.

As he felt a huge, red-sparking emotion flow through him, as he felt a tremble and a jitter, he told himself: maybe it was just exhaustion from the day's labour. Or it was the plan he'd obsessed over for so long finally coming together. Or the romantic slant of the low sun's light.

Or maybe, he cautiously let himself realise, it was none of these things—maybe he was just experiencing the truth: that this boat was glorious in ways he could not fully comprehend. That its golden hue was overbearing in its richness. That the way its neat design caused it to slice through the air, even as it lay stationary, was somehow savagely beautiful. The boat seemed to lunge towards the river, as if running home.

Compounding all this was something else he had not expected: the stripped wood's aroma. Now that the stale, petrol-like scent of the paint was gone, Ned was hit by a spicy, sappy pine smell, somehow both cleansing and intoxicating, subtle and strong. It was entirely new to him, and it was unavoidable. At first he thought a lubricant had leaked onto his tools, or that Maggie had spilled perfume on his clothes. It was only when he lowered his face to the boat that he realised it was coming from the timber, rising from the grains to settle in his nose and throat.

He had never worked closely with wood before. If he'd thought of it as having a smell at all, it had been as the broad scent of the forest: the pungency of rotting vegetation, the clearing menthol of eucalypt, the off-sweet tang of wild blossoms, the dankness of mud, the freshness of rain, the rot of a dead wallaby, the chalky minerality of broken rock. The odours of trees belonged to their leaves and flowers; he'd assumed timber would be mute. He wondered at his wrongness, as the wood spice filled his lungs, sank into his blood.

The sight and smell. He felt tricked, drunk. He hadn't known the world could do things like this to him.

~

He would have gone to find Jackbird if Jackbird hadn't found him first. Ned was wiping down the shed the next day when his friend came into view, crunching along the beach. When Jackbird saw the boat, he stopped. His face was a palette of circles. 'Look at the bloody thing, Neddy.'

Ned wanted to shrug. Wanted to pass the boat off as ordinary, not worth making a fuss over. But Jackbird's face and voice confirmed that it wasn't just him, that it really was something else, something terrific, and then he was smiling, showing teeth.

'Come up all right, I guess.'

'I'll say.' Jackbird was walking around the boat, touching it, whistling. He sniffed. 'What kind of wood is this?'

'Not sure.'

Jackbird kept circling. Paused at the stern. 'Gonna need a rudder.'

'Seems that way.'

Jackbird's face softened, his eyes sliding upwards. Ned knew what was happening. Soon Jackbird was telling him how they would steal a rudder from the boatyard in Beaconsfield. How they'd take his father's truck and go there at night, how they'd slice through the fence with bolt cutters, how they'd remove a rudder from one of those fancy French boats with screwdrivers and wrenches, how they'd muffle the sound of it all with feed sacks.

Ned let him finish. Let him get carried away. Then said that he'd probably just make one. They argued for a while, without much bite—they were both too taken with the boat's shine to concentrate on anything else—before agreeing that they'd at least go inspect the rudders up close.

They took their bikes, rushing up the road. At the boatyard Ned made for the coloured dinghies while Jackbird went to distract the owner.

Ned walked down the rows of boats, thinking of how

he'd felt the last time he'd done this, of the despair he'd felt at the prices. He kept going until he found a dinghy close in size and design to his own. He bent over its stern, staring closely at the rudder. Studied its shape, the heft of its stock, the swoop of its blade. The way it was attached to the hull and tiller. He took out a notebook and pencil and began to sketch, noting the dimensions, the way each piece related to the others in size and connection.

A whistle brought him away from the page. Jackbird was coming towards him. The owner of the boatyard hung in the background, arms crossed. Jackbird stopped at Ned's side.

'Time to go, mate. He's had enough of me.'

Ned took a last long look at the rudder, then followed Jackbird's quick steps out of the yard. The owner watched them go through the gate and out into the street, until they were on their bikes, zipping down the road.

Jackbird was buoyed. 'I told that fella about your boat. He said it sounds like it's made of Huon pine.' He grinned. 'He also said I was full of it. Said there's no way you found a Huon pine dinghy in a junkyard.'

Ned didn't know what to make of this. He thought of the sketch in his pocket. Let Jackbird worry about talk and speculation.

~

Back at home he began cobbling together a rudder out of planks leftover from the supply he'd used to build the shed. At first it seemed straightforward: saw pieces into shape, nail and glue them together, emulate the rudder he'd sketched in the boat-yard. But he couldn't achieve the right shape; the planks were of varying widths, and no matter how carefully he measured them against each other, he couldn't cut them into complementary segments. Chiselling their ends after they'd been sawn made it worse. He had no aptitude for the delicacy of the work, the carefulness of it. Toothy wounds splintered all over his creations.

He tried tracing an outline of a rudder on the floor of the shed, so he had a guide to cut against. This made planning easier, although his sawing refused to improve. Eventually he thought he'd brought something useful together, something that might work. But when he lifted it from the floor he saw that it was misshapen and ugly. The combination of its planks had looked sound, but when tested against gravity they began to come undone. Light showed through wide gaps. The nails holding it together creaked against cracked apertures.

He was holding the rough mess of it in his hands when Jackbird returned, now in the company of his father. They were approaching the shore through the scrub. With them was Ned's own father. Ned put down his tools. Straightened up. Thought about saying something, but didn't. Chose to let the boat speak for itself.

Both fathers went straight to the shed. Jackbird's rubbed his chin, whistled like his son had, swore that it couldn't be the same boat they'd seen at Falmouth's. Ned's father only lifted an eyebrow. After their inspection they agreed that the boat seller was right: the wood could only be Huon pine. It must have come from the far southwest, the only place it grew, a great rough place of screaming winds and wilderness kings. The best kind of wood for building boats on the planet, Jackbird's father said. Ancient and slow-growing, uncorruptible by salt or water, impervious to the attention of insects, ever moist with oils that repelled all elements. Not a true pine, as definitions went, but something older and rarer. A species whose trees could live for thousands of years, if axes and fire didn't find them. A light timber, almost airy in weight, that nosed through water like a hunting shark. A treasured material only master builders were given access to. Loggers had another name for it: green gold.

Jackbird's father again ran his eyes over the boat, laid his hands on its body. Inhaled its spice. Turned to Ned's father, and when he saw that his neighbour had looked away to the river, that William West wasn't really there anymore, switched his attention to Ned. An urgent question pulsed from his expression: Did you know? Did you?

Ned wanted to shrug, shake his head, to communicate that it was all a fluke. But in the knocking of his blood he knew that wasn't true. He'd seen the flash of colour beneath the peeling paint. He'd chased it through layers of off-green muck. He hadn't known what he would find, but he had known, somehow, that it would be worth revealing. The boat had told him. He had just followed its directions.

~

The rudder would need to come from a single piece of timber. Ned hadn't read this in a book or heard it from a salt-skinned shipwright; his own ineptitude demanded it. Nails couldn't weaken or ruin the rudder if there were no nails involved.

Eucalypts were plentiful, eucalypts of many kinds, but they were too hard and would tear the teeth from his saw. He began to hunt for softer timber. The valley was filled with blue-green gums and knobbly coastal natives, but after two days of wood-watching he found an old oak stump down the road from Limberlost, near the convent. It had not been dug up or burnt out. It was wide and not too old; the tree had only been removed the previous spring, when the nuns had been worried it would come down in a storm and crush their tomatoes. Ned looked around, searching for wimpled sisters. When he didn't see any he took a saw to the stump, cut a thin round off the top, then another, wider round from the fresher wood beneath. He heaved the latter onto its side and began rolling it down the road, down the driveway, all the way down the property and through the bush to the boatshed, where he lifted it onto a hobby horse.

He got to work with care, with hesitation, with pencil and saw and chisel. At first he worried he was butchering it, that he didn't have the skill to cut it correctly, that the result would be the same as with the planks. But after a while it seemed to be coming together. Shavings and offcuts crowded around his feet, and something like a rudder began to emerge from the oak.

He stepped back, viewing the slab of timber. Took in the neatness of it, imagined it wave-licked, river-wet. Then he returned to his work, snagged his chisel in a knot, and in his impatience to remove the tool managed to split the wood down the grain.

For a while he swore at the rent timber. Then he flung it into the paperbarks and walked back to the oak stump, where he cut off another round. His previous efforts had lowered its height, and to free this third slab he had to lie flat on the ground, easing his saw back and forth, his shoulder and hip hard against the dirt. Again he turned the wheel of wood on its side. Again he rolled it to the boatshed.

He repeated the same process, this time taking it slower, taking more care. Guiding his tools with soft fear. He put down his chisel much earlier in the process this time, using sandpaper instead. Grinding it over bumps, exhausting his arm. Leaking sweat onto sawdust. When he thought it looked finished he used a hand drill to bore a hole in the spot where it would attach to the boat.

He worried that it wouldn't fit, but when he lifted it to the stern it slid in well enough, and once he had fastened it with an old bolt it hung more or less like he had hoped it would. The swivelling mechanism was sound; the short tiller he'd attached it to was easy to grip. And despite his worry that it would stand out, that it would look poor and dull next to the Huon pine, its deeper colour contrasted neatly against the straw-gold boat planks. A dark exclamation in all that brightness.

Next he took a wider eye to the hull, looking for holes, searching for where the river would push through. He found no gaps, but didn't trust his limited knowledge. He did not want to push the boat into the water and watch it dive to the sand, so he decided to seal the hull. The wood was rough after the scouring, anyway, in need of some kind of finishing agent. He was tempted to varnish the whole thing, to slop glossy oil all over it, as he'd seen his father do to wooden furniture. But he couldn't bring himself to stain the Huon like that; it seemed like the sort of act a person would be arrested for. Instead he applied only a thin, colourless veneer of shellac. It gave the timber a light gleam under direct sunlight, a smoother touch and a sealed skin—nothing more. There were larger gaps, higher up the sides, which would not be under threat on a calm surface but might betray him during a storm. He patched them with tar—black winks of comfort.

He repaired the bench seat with offcuts of the rudder, nails, shellac and more tar. For the broken oar, he whittled a new handle from a she-oak pole. Then the boat was missing only a sail. He wanted to take it out anyway, to row it, to test it. Thought he might take Jackbird, but changed his mind; if something went wrong, Jackbird's crowing and cavorting wouldn't help. It would just be him. Just Ned and the boat and the river, preparing for the moment his brothers came home and saw him out there, alone and masterful. He thought of Toby watching him from the beach, smiling wide, skimming a rock over the wavelets. Thought of Bill standing there too, looming tall. His face a cloud.

# 13

IMAGINING HIS BROTHERS seeing him on the river sent Ned a memory from years earlier, when Bill had gone to help a friend find a lost ram. This friend's farm was a few valleys over, near Mount Roland. Bill could not yet drive, so he'd got a lift with a classmate. Their father had been in Beaconsfield for the day. Maggie had told Bill not to go, but he had ignored her. Ned remembered it clearly: Bill climbing into a truck that had pulled up at the end of the driveway as he and Toby watched from the porch, while Maggie turned her back on all three of them.

Bill returned three days later. Fell out of the truck, limped to the house. Didn't say what had happened. Ned found that out at school, from people who knew the family of Bill's friend. The ram had gone missing from a far paddock at the start of Roland's slope, during the hardest part of a hard winter. This hard winter had followed a hard autumn, summer, spring—a bad year. A bad time to lose a ram. So even though the men and boys were sure the animal had frozen to death or slipped from a snowy crag, they struck into the trees and up the trails anyway, holding their collars to their necks.

They split up, pushing through the rising forest of tree ferns and eucalypts for a whole day. Found nothing, not even a strand of wool snagged on a branch. The second day, the search party had halved. The remaining searchers crashed through the forest at dawn and met steep dolerite cliffs, grey and severe in the breaking light. Cutting them apart were gullies and trails, usually easily traversable but now sheeted with snow, sheened with ice. Two members of the party were assigned to each gully. Bill went with his friend, to the farthest gap in the cliffs. They were the ones who found the ram.

It was said at Ned's school that it appeared to them suddenly, violently. They were wading through the snow, their legs plunging to knee depth with each step. Bill was ahead of his friend, so he first heard the crashing noise coming from the ledge above them. He thought it was a boulder, loosened by the wind, but when he looked up he saw the ram, rushing down from a rocky peak, its dirty cream wool blending into the white snow and grey sky.

It was coming straight at them, its curled horns lowered to the height of their guts. Bill's friend dived into the snow, but Bill stayed still. Took in a gulp of mountain air. Met the ram's charge in a braced hunch, let its skull smash into his sternum as he caught a horn in each hand. A wet, sickening crack reverberated around the mountain. The impact rocked him, but he stayed upright, either through strength and skill or because he was sunk so deep into the snow he couldn't be moved.

Bill held the ram by the horns as it fought him. His friend

climbed up from the snow and watched as Bill wrestled the furious creature, countering each of its assaults with a grim refusal to yield ground. It snorted, strained, butted at him, tried to impale him, tried to bite him. Bill was grunting. His face was crimson, his breaths ragged. His grip started to weaken. But when the ram's legs wobbled he bent his knees, found a point of leverage and, with a tremendous heave, twisted the ram's horns and wrenched it to the ground. It lay flipped on its side, its shuddering breaths melting the snow around its nose.

Bill gathered himself. Waited for his arms to stop shaking. Touched the bloody stamp on his chest where the ram's charge had struck him. Then he and his friend trussed the beast's legs and dragged it back to the farm, where they warmed it back to life in front of an orange fire.

That was the story getting around Ned's school. Most people believed it. But it was disputed by some younger students, one of whom claimed to have been part of the search party. His version of events held that Bill's friend had been the one to find the animal, and that it was not in a state of fury or madness but in distress. Thin bleats had reached Bill's friend's ears, and he had followed the noise until he found the ram lying still, swaddled by snow. He saw that two of its legs were wedged in a fissure in the rock. The hooves were stuck tight. Rime slicked each shank.

Bill's friend grabbed the ram by the curl of its horns and began trying to pull it free. The hours in the snow had left the animal exhausted, so it did not fight or resist. But its legs were jammed, possibly frozen onto the rock as well as being stuck, and Bill's friend couldn't get it to budge. He heaved, he hauled, he huffed white steam. He worked different angles, but it would not loosen. The ram blinked at him, not bothering to bleat now, not even when Bill's friend tugged so hard that the rock bit into its trapped flesh, freeing blood onto the snow, onto the frost, warm red trickles that froze before they could run or pool.

Bill's friend collapsed next to the ram, swearing and panting. These noises reached Bill, who had just begun ascending the track. He shuffled through the snow to his friend's side and took in the scene. Gazed at the ram. Circled it. Leaned in to inspect the hard-stuck legs. Looked the creature in the black line of its eye. Measured its panicked breaths. Laced his fingers into its wool, hunting for heat.

He then—if Ned's schoolmate was to be believed—began speaking to the ram. Soft murmurs that his friend couldn't make out. The ram's breathing steadied. Bill kept talking to it, his lips close to its soft ear, as he pulled from his pocket a handful of green winter grass that he'd ripped from a paddock that dawn. Now he blew a warm breath onto the bright blades and held them beneath the ram's nose. Waved his hand back and forth. Used the other one to rub life into its legs. Kept whispering to it, kept offering the grass until the ram began to wriggle. It strained, squirmed, repositioned. Kicked at the rock. Kicked hard. Kicked itself free and fell onto Bill's chest. Lay in his arms, weak as a lamb, chewing at the grass as Bill carried it all the way down the bitter slope.

It was a long way back. It was so cold, and snow was settling on Bill's arms and hands, so he didn't notice when the ram cooled and died—not until he reached the flatness of the paddock, where he could walk more steadily and feel the awful stiffness of the animal in his grip. Over the paddock he could see lights glowing through farmhouse windows, warm and welcome.

# 14

WITH THIS STORY in mind, Ned felt even more compelled to test the boat alone—to prepare for the moment Bill and Toby would come home and see him taming the river. But as he pushed the boat onto the shore he looked back at the shed's rafters and remembered what his father had told him.

Maggie came without question. She'd known he'd bought a boat, that he'd been working on it. These things could not be hidden on the orchard. But she hadn't spoken to him about it, and Ned, still sore from how little she'd given him in response to his heroism over the mare, had not brought it up with her.

'Would you like to come out in my boat,' he'd said. She didn't say anything; she just wiped her forehead with the back of her wrist, took off her gardening gloves and followed him to the waterline.

He'd laid she-oak poles between the shed and the river as runners. She helped him push the boat over them, although the curious lightness of the timber meant the task really only needed one person. Across the sand it ran, into the river. Immediately it drifted away from them, eager to float. Ned caught it with a snatching hand. Maggie swung herself on board. He pushed off and copied her leap, ungainly with the thrill of it.

He scrabbled for the oars. Maggie was already sitting in the bow, craning her head over the side. Ned put the blades into the water, began hurriedly paddling. Realised soon that he didn't need to. They weren't going anywhere; they were meandering, testing the boat's capabilities.

Ned pushed down on the oar handles, raising them into the air. Let himself breathe. Felt the rhythm of the river in his thighs, his stomach. Told himself that it was happening: that all those punctured pelts and bloody mornings had been worth it.

They drifted towards the river's centre. The wind played with his hair, not as forcefully as he'd dreamed it would, but still it was present: a fresh hand on his face. There was so much fizz in his head he thought he might fall overboard. He nearly let out a wild shout, but was worried that a burst of feeling like that might lead to an undamming of other emotions. He did not want to cry in front of Maggie. Then he noticed that she already was.

She was doing it noiselessly, but the tears on her face were thick, and her face was hazed red. Ned waited for her to stop, but she kept at it, her shoulders jerking. The weight of saying and doing nothing became too great for him.

'You all right?'

She looked at him, her face wet. 'Of course I'm all right.'

Ned turned away. Fumbled for words. 'Is it your friend? The one in the navy?'

Maggie coughed. Dipped a hand in the river. The coolness of the water seemed to steady her, and her breaths began to even out. 'No. As far as I'm aware, he's fine. The reports haven't mentioned anything about the North Sea in weeks. They've got them on the run in Europe.' She dragged an arm across her nose and cheeks. 'Have you been reading them?'

Ned baulked. 'Some of them. Most of them.'

'And what have you learned?'

'Not much. What you said: they've got them on the run.'

'In Europe.'

'Yes. In Europe.'

Ned felt the heat of the implication. He didn't know what to do with that knowledge. Hadn't known what to do all summer.

'Other families are getting letters, you know.' Maggie was twisting her fingers through the current.

'Other families?'

'Of the men who were in Singapore. The ones who were redeployed, or injured, or captured. Letters are arriving.'

Ned hadn't known that. Had thought there had been no word at all, and that this lack of correspondence was just as likely a good thing as bad. He let this new truth filter through him, felt the sucking dread of it. Felt, for a few moments, like he might pour himself into the river.

Sometime later Maggie cuffed a wavelet, broke the silence. 'Mum loved being on the water. Did you know that?'

Ned roused himself. 'No.'

'Sailing, mostly. She went to the Lake District as a child, where she learned how. Best time of her life, she told me once. But she rowed as well. That's how she met Dad. She was at sculling practice one morning and he was helping unload a shipment of apples. When she was coming past the dock, he spilled a case into the river. The apples bobbed towards Mum's boat, and she had to stop and wait as he fished them out with a net. She said he was being clumsy, but Dad always maintained it was deliberate. That's what he used to say about it. A well-placed case of apples.'

Ned had heard his father say it before: *Nothing like a well-placed case of apples*. He had thought it a simple expression about getting on with your neighbours, about the importance of friendly gestures. He'd never thought it had anything to do with his mother. Her name flashed into his mind: Liesel. The thought of her as a young woman, rowing down flat freshwater, jolted him. He'd grown used to thinking of her as a parent, as a wife. As dead.

Maggie's hand was still in the river, her fingers ripping through the water. 'She had a little yacht she used to take me out on. Bill too, though he wouldn't remember. He could barely walk.' She began to cry again, this time with audible sobs. She gripped the side of the dinghy, her hands pale and tight on the Huon pine.

'Afterwards Dad sold it to someone up at the river mouth.' She watched the clouds sliding through the sky. 'You really need to get a sail.'

# 15

YEARS LATER, SHORTLY after Ned's third daughter, Harriet, was born—four years after Grace had followed Sally into the world—news reached the valley of new technologies that had been developed in the orchards of Britain. The local orchardists agreed that they needed access to this knowledge, that in an international market they and their crops could not be left behind. Writing letters would not be enough. Someone needed to go there, to talk to the flat-capped farmers of the western counties and wring from them the necessary information about these innovations.

It made sense for the valley's representative to be Jackbird. He had led the way into the Japanese market. He had the words, the smile, the velvet. But he had broken his leg after rolling a tractor he'd recently bought, a new model that he had no idea how to operate. The other orchardists all had excuses too, or were at least quick to declare themselves incapable of the journey. Ned's orchard was still the smallest in the valley—the only one modest enough for the other growers to keep an eye on while also tending to their own.

And so Ned went to England. The first time he travelled overseas, his flights paid for with money pooled by his fellow orchardists. When asked, years later, how he justified leaving his wife so soon after she'd given birth, he was unable to come up with a good answer. It was just what we did then, he would say, or that it had to be done, or that he wasn't just doing it for himself, while knowing none of those things were exactly true. Always, at these times, he thought of their growing orchard, the vast spread of their vegetable garden, bountiful but also beautiful thanks to the roses and tulips his wife had threaded through the beds. The look on her face when he'd told her about the trip. The old boldness as she asked him what he was waiting for, said that of course he had to go, even as her face was softened by sorrow she wouldn't admit to.

He landed in the south, rented a car, drove northwest. Was unprepared for the greenness of the place. Meadows, trees, hedges, all thick and wet, all a deep, storybook green under a mottled grey sky. Green and grey everywhere, interrupted only by villages of stone houses, cobbled roads and looming taverns. Rain came in drifts, in dribbles, always falling. He pushed through the foreignness of it all.

At the orchard he'd been sent to he met three middle-aged men who took him through the mizzle to the heart of their apple groves. There, with friendly patience, they revealed to him their wondrous innovation: a spray. A combination of insecticide and fungicide, stronger and more durable than any other in existence, able to protect all apple varieties from every kind of pestilence. They showed him how to dilute it, how to decant it into the mist-spraying device, how to attach that device to a tractor, how to aim the machine at the top of the trees, which allowed the death-cloud to fall and coat every part of the foliage and fruit. Through the groves they rolled, mist rising and falling in their wake.

Ned had seen sprays before. Every orchardist he'd ever known had mixed copper sulphate in their sheds, doused it across their crop. But these West Anglians swore to him that this chemical's effectiveness was unparalleled. They showed him their evidence: swollen, healthy crops, and ledgers spitting rude profits.

'Just make sure the wife has the washing in before you start spraying,' they told him. 'It can make a horrible mess on your clothes.'

They gave him the details of the tiny collective that manufactured it, the address from which it could be ordered. Told him what to say, who to talk to. Ned thanked them. He gave them specimens and cuttings from his own orchard, which he had brought as gifts. He ate dinner in one of their houses, asked the right questions, spoke a little about what it was like to grow fruit in the southern hemisphere. Afterwards, wrecked by travel, he fell asleep on a cot one of their wives had made up for him in a small study.

In the morning he thanked them again over a hot breakfast, and left. But once he was off the property, he pulled over. He had no destination. The orchardists back home hadn't known how long it would take him to learn and master the new technology, so his flight was still days away. He pulled out the map the rental company had given him. Dragged his eyes across Britain's pale shape. Didn't want to go to any of the cities any more than he wanted to visit the cities of the antipodes, where crowds pressed him, the volume of life felt heavy, and not being able to see the horizon meant he could never settle. He kept looking. Didn't see the point in going to a beach. Thought of going to see the Roman ruins, the old wall they'd stapled across the island. Felt attracted to the age of it, the massive stretch of time separating his own life from theirs. While searching for Hadrian's name, he saw the Lake District. Studied the map's key. Saw that he wasn't far away.

He pushed north into a higher kind of country: taller trees, steeper hills, all still insistently green. The road curled and doglegged: sharper angles than he was used to. As he climbed, the forest petered out and he came to be surrounded on all sides by rich paddocks, dotted all over with black-faced sheep. Ancient stone fences cut the land into a rough grid. The sky was close. Up the road twisted, until it peaked in a saddle between two grassy peaks, before shooting down into a field of huge, shining lakes.

He had, up to that point, expected very little of the British landscape. Had thought of it as a mountainless, beachless, heat-less place where tweeded farmers shot pheasants and children were always going on picnics. Had thought its greyness and greenness to be emblematic of all this. But now he saw these lakes, pocked through a rugged country of dramatic hills. He began to understand why his mother had loved it here.

Ned coasted to one of the little towns, found a room in a pub with low ceilings, moustached men, and a large fire with a group of border collies steaming on its hearth. Felt like he'd fallen through time.

In the morning he found a man who agreed to take him out on the water. They cast off from the pier onto Lake Windermere. Ned helped the man raise the sail, and for a few hours they coasted about, taking in the contours of the lake. The man told Ned about the others: Ullswater, Grasmere, Coniston Water, Buttermere. Fairytale names to Ned. From the water, the hills—fells, the man called them—were even larger, more dramatic. Oak, ash and red-berried rowans dominated their lower slopes, ceding the heights to grass and sheep and stone. The wind was light. There were no waves.

It was so calm, in the way that calmness can feel transcendental, but Ned felt cold and glum. He'd missed his wife and daughters from the moment he boarded the first plane. Felt a constant ache of regret. He worried he'd done the wrong thing, while knowing the other orchardists wouldn't have forgiven him if he'd refused. He felt in his mind for Sally's little grasps, the fumbling hooks of Grace's fingers. The slow blink of fresh little Harriet. Saw the eldest two shrieking under the falling water of a hose he'd turned on them in the garden. Remembered the look on his wife's face, hard and beautiful. He thought too of the knowledge he was bringing home, and the benefits it might have for his family and his community. But it did not console him; he saw only the orchard he was not on, the daughters he was not with, and he came to realise that he was behaving in the manner of so many men he knew and had known and had rarely respected: as a work-loving loner in the false skin of a family man.

He shook his head, tried to listen to what the sailor was telling him about the wind and the currents. He couldn't do anything for his family until he got home. He should enjoy this place while he was here. This place he was unlikely to ever see again, this place that Maggie had told him his mother had loved.

The man kept talking, pointing out rock formations on the hillsides, ancient places where armoured knights once skewered dragons, and Ned allowed himself to think of what his life might have been like if his mother hadn't died a few months after he was born. Usually he didn't think of her in relation to himself. He just imagined a version of her based on what he'd heard from others: a quiet, sporty woman of high talent, slanted humour, good hair. He closed his eyes and heard the name Liesel being called across paddocks, across waterways. Voices high and flushed.

It was a light sketch of a person, because that was all he had to go on. But here, on this English lake so far from home, he caught himself wishing that she was there with him, whatever the truth of her had been. He wanted to know why she'd liked it here so much. It was a striking place, but he wanted to know what exactly had struck her. Was it the rising, plummeting fells? Was it the grey-shining water? The Robin Hood forests? The Beatrix Potter villages? The feeling of timelessness? Was it Windermere she'd learned to sail on, or one of the other lakes? Was he drifting on water that had once held her reflection?

Most of all he wished she could see him, out there on the sailboat. He wished she had been able to know that he'd come to this place. That her pale, squirming son had grown into a man who could sail like she could. He wished she could watch him on this water, the way he'd wanted Bill and Toby to watch him on his little dinghy, all those years ago on the shores of Limberlost. Wanted someone on land to come back to.

The wind picked up. The temperature dropped. The rest of the day passed quickly as Ned helped the man wrangle the sail and steer the boat back to the jetty. That night Ned bought him dinner at the same pub where he was staying. Some of the man's friends met them there, insisting that Ned try the local beer, the local pie. These other men were also sailors. Soon they were talking about their boats, their lakes, the things they'd done and seen on water.

To Ned their stories were both strange and familiar, and a good distraction from how he'd felt out on Windermere. After two pints he'd stopped imagining his mother, stopped condemning himself as a failed father and husband, and felt ready to slide into the talk, to tell them about the boat he'd bought and restored as a teenager. His hidden treasure of Huon pine. The quiet spell of it. What it had meant to him back then: the feeling that had flowed in the wake of all that green gold. He bought another round. Thought he had his words lined straight.

But back at the table, the conversation had shifted. Now the men were discussing the creatures they'd caught: all kinds of fish, from all kinds of waters. Trout and chub, sweet-fleshed grayling and fighting salmon. Hulking barbel and wolfish pike. Ocean fish too: rod-snapping cod, enormous white seabass, halibut bigger than a man. Monsters, the sailors said.

Ned, whose thoughts had tailed off before this fish-bragging entered saltwater, felt himself surge awake. 'Monsters?'

And then he was away, words spilling, words running. You think you know monsters? he asked them. Have you ever met one? Have you sailed at night to a river mouth guarded by a leviathan? Have you seen its hump rear from the waves, a hump bigger than your boat? Have you reached for your brothers as you saw stars reflecting from a harpoon that had lanced into its blubbery head and snapped off in the wet meat of its brain? Have you screamed your throat numb? Have you seen the broad wedge of its tail erupt into the night, rising with hideous power to hang above your father's head? Have you waited, starlit and voiceless, for its heavy flukes to fall? In all your grey-green lives, have you ever known a terror like that?

# 16

BY THE TIME Ned had his boat on the river the summer was at its peak. All the creeks were dry, the troughs parched, the ponds empty. Moisture had steamed off even the moss. Rain was needed, but none came. Possums fell from trees, wallabies folded into piles of heavy fur. All this hot flesh summoned scavengers. The nights rang with the screams of feeding devils, and the daylight skies were dotted with hawks, more appearing each day, scanning the valley for the summer's latest victim, so many hawks and eagles as well, wedge-tailed eagles as big as mastiffs, and under the clouds of these circling raptors Callie finally steeled her body, steeled her mind, raised her shotgun and squeezed the trigger.

The barrel exploded in her grip. The stock flew backwards, smashing into the shoulder she had braced for the impact. But the recoil was stronger than she'd expected, strong enough to kick the ball of her arm clean out of its socket.

Ned heard about it from Maggie, who'd taken some of her

old schoolbooks to Callie that morning, thinking they might still be on the curriculum. She told Ned outside the house, while he was digging dirt out of the tread of his boots with a screwdriver.

'Completely dislocated it. Lots of bruising. She's in pain.' Maggie indicated her own shoulder. Circled a large patch of her shirt.

Ned put down the screwdriver. 'Is she in hospital?'

'At home. The doctor's been.'

Ned imagined the horse-kick of the impact. Pictured Callie lying in the paddock, exposed to the sun, shadowed only by high wings.

'Did she hit it?'

Maggie's face scrunched. 'Hit what?'

'The hawk.'

'I didn't ask.' She made to leave, but stopped in the doorway. 'You better go see her.'

There was a particularly stubborn piece of grit in the heel of Ned's left boot. He'd been working at it for what felt like ten minutes before his sister had arrived. Now he turned the screwdriver back on it, levering and wrenching.

Maggie rubbed at her eyes. 'Dad's right.' She left him on the porch, flakes of dirt falling onto burning cement. 'The things you don't know.'

~

Ned washed, scrubbed, dried himself. What he should do next came to him over a pile of soap bubbles. It was obvious, unavoidable. A course of action that wasn't so much a choice as a necessity.

146

His boots were now free of clinging chunks, so when he walked next door he felt fast and light, even with a heavy object in his arms. Jackbird and his father were in the paddock, and his mother was chopping green wood in preparation for a winter that felt impossible to imagine in the roar of summer, but would eventually arrive with frost and darkness. Ned waved to her. Let himself into the house.

He'd been there many times, but had never entered Callie's room. He wasn't even sure where it was. He called her name, and a noise came through a door down the hall. He knocked, went in. She was lying in bed, a sheet pulled up to her waist. Her arm was in a white sling. A large purple bruise splashed out onto her collarbone from under her shirt.

Ned felt awkward, like he shouldn't have come. He stared at her arm. 'That doesn't look good.'

She looked at the wall, at her lap. 'No good,' she eventually agreed. 'But the doctor said I'll be all right in a few weeks.' She glanced down at her mottled skin. 'Hurts like hell, though.'

'I bet.' He looked around the room. Realised he might be prying, turned his attention to the world outside the window. 'Did you hit it?'

Callie sat up. 'No.' Life in her face. 'The gun kicked up. Missed by a mile.'

Ned felt something within his chest relax. Callie shifted, winced. As she moved, she noticed the crate under Ned's arm. Her eyes went wide.

Ned lowered it to the wooden floor. 'Thought it might cheer you up.' He made sure the door was closed. He checked the window, closed the drawers and cupboards of Callie's wardrobe.

Then he removed the tin lid from the crate and stepped back.

The quoll's nose twitched up. Whiskers vibrating in the air. Its front paws latched onto the side of the crate, and it pulled the front half of its body over the side. Eyes dark and wet and large, blinking, adjusting to the light. Rich fur, twisting muscle. It lunged out of the crate and onto the floor. Callie ripped in a breath.

This course of action, which had felt so right an hour earlier, was now revealing itself to Ned as idiotic. The quoll could do anything in this room. He waited for it to try to escape, to slash the curtains and sheets, to scream, to turn its claws and teeth onto him. But it only sniffed at its surroundings, and began gingerly padding about. Brushing its whiskers across every-thing, flinching and turning on the floorboards. There was a slight limp to its injured leg, but it did not stop it from leaping onto the bed, where it nosed at Callie's feet, before climbing higher, onto a bookcase.

Callie's face had blanched. She and Ned watched it move, taking in the fullness of it. The glow and shine of its brown-cream pelt. The long stretch of its tail. The soft art with which it moved.

Once the quoll had toured the room and was beginning to scratch furrows in the windowsill, Ned took a duck egg and some dried rabbit from his pocket. Clicked his fingers. The quoll turned, raised its nose. He showed it the egg. It came towards him, and when he put the egg and meat into the crate it climbed in. He slapped the lid back on. Huffed with relief.

Callie was rigid, bewitched. After a moment she said: 'It looks better.'

They heard its teeth crunch. The quoll still filled the room, even though it was no longer in sight.

Ned laid a hand on the lid. 'Once the limp's gone, so is it.'

Callie looked at the crate. Then at him: straight at him.

~

The river didn't live to be paddled on, and his boat wasn't built to be manhandled. He discovered this on his second voyage, dragging the oars through heavy water, going slow, going not far until a current took over and he had to fight it, to heave the boat back to near the shore before he lost total control. It wasn't optimal; it wasn't what he'd dreamed of. Maggie was right. He needed a sail.

He took his bike into Beaconsfield, a bag filled with the last of his rabbit pelts strapped to his back. Went straight to Singline's. Expected the usual price, the usual speed of transaction. But from the moment he entered, Singline looked at him differently. A narrowness to his eyes, coyness on his busted old face. He drew out the talk, the bartering, the game of it. Ned grew exasperated. Singline fiddled with the pelts, rubbing at the fur with an expression of false thoughtfulness. Finally, in a careless, almost distracted voice, he said: 'I heard you've bought a boat.'

Coldness on Ned's neck. 'That's right.'

Singline smiled at him. 'I wondered what you were going to do with all that money I've been giving you.'

'Giving?'

'Trading. Now don't get uppity.' Singline kept smiling, amused by something unseen and unsaid. 'You worked hard. Those rabbits didn't trap themselves.'

He seemed to be waiting for Ned to respond. When he didn't, Singline kept talking. 'Quite a nice boat, I'm told. Huon pine. You don't see many of those these days. Who would've thought old Falmouth would be hiding a thing like that.'

Ned kept still. Kept himself from reacting. He wanted to demand who'd told him, but knew Singline wouldn't give a straight answer. He pointed at the pile of fur. 'There's nothing wrong with these.'

'Not at all.' Singline turned the pelt in his hand, as if remembering it was there. 'I'm just pondering things, Master West. Pondering why you're still trying to sell me rabbit skins when we all know the war is winding down, and the army isn't going to need many more hats. When you've already bought your little boat.'

Ned was aware he had crossed his arms, aware his frustration wasn't helping him. Singline seemed happy to wait. His dirty thumb in the plush fibres of Ned's work.

'I need a sail.'

Again Singline smiled, now with his mouth open, almost chuckling. 'You Wests. We could've got through this so much quicker if you knew how to explain yourself.' He put the pelt down and wandered to the back of the store, returning with a bundle of off-white cloth. It was folded up, but Ned saw eyelets stitched into its corner. A price tag had been looped through one of them.

'I don't think we even need to involve currency. Your pelts for this fine sail. You couldn't ask for a better deal.' Singline patted the cloth, summoning up a puff of dust. 'What serendipity.'

Ned read the tag, calculated the price he'd usually get for a stack of pelts. Realised he was being cheated.

'Deal.' He picked up the sail and began to leave. His anger was dying even before he'd reached the door. The material was heavy and stiff in his arms. Already he was imagining hoisting it. Already he could see the wind rushing into it, uncreasing it, ballooning it.

'Young West.' Ned turned back. Saw Singline settling into his chair. A different look was on him now, one Ned hadn't seen before. A kind of contemplation, even sadness. Ned didn't like it. Only manners stopped him from leaving.

'I imagine you aren't going to hear this from anyone else. So.' Singline paused. Wrestled with his mouth. 'Well done. You've put in a good shift. I hope you look after that boat, and that it looks after you.' He raised a hand in something like a salute.

Ned was red-cheeked, wrong-footed. Zipped up tight. All he could manage was to nod and cough.

Outside he let the sun burn the encounter out of him. He tied the sail to his handlebars, began to ride. As he rolled down the main street, he saw his father exiting the bank. Ned began to pedal towards him. He forgot Singline's unexpected sincerity, if that's what it had been; he wanted to tell his father about the sail.

As he got nearer he was about to call out, but something in the way his father was standing made him stop. He saw how still the old man was. How he was not shading his eyes from the sun but had them closed, and was breathing deeply and slowly, breathing like it was his job. When his father finally opened his eyes and began walking down the street, Ned didn't follow him.

Instead he sped back to Limberlost, unbalanced by the weight of the sail, unbalanced by men who could not stay steady.

~

Ropes in the shed, ropes in the attic, ropes in old apple netting. Ropes coiled into loops, ropes looped in on themselves. Soft ropes, unused for years, maybe never used, probably bought when Limberlost was bigger and more fruitful. Ropes of all lengths and girths. All the rigging he needed.

He didn't know how to tie on the sail, how to configure it properly. So he cycled past the nearby jetties that lanced out from the shoreline. He studied the yachts and boats moored at each one, taking note of where and how their sails sat, were tied, were folded. A consistency of design began to emerge: the places where the mainsail met the boom and mast, where the backstay was tied to the transom.

Out on the water he saw yachts at work, not dormant like their moored cousins but awake, dancing, alive. He saw how theirs jibs swooped towards the bow. How they swung around to catch the push of the wind. He drew these sights in, stamped them in his thoughts, stamped hard enough so that he was able to go back to his boatshed and attach his sail in a way that looked right.

It was too big; there was too much material; it hung on the rigging like a listless ghost. He took it down, wondered at the problem. He decided to cut out the eyelets, trim the sail around its borders, then restitch them. The cutting went fine—he used measuring tape and a sharp knife—but the stitching proved more difficult.

Eventually he went to Maggie, asked for help. She smiled

in a way that made Ned feel she was laughing at him, that he was foolish, but she brought her sewing kit to the boatshed and showed him how it was done. How to push a needle, how to drag a thread. When he was finished he hoisted it high. It hung better. Not perfectly, but with a pleasing tautness he hoped would stand up to the wind's strength.

And then: to the waterline. Into the dinghy, onto the river. An hour of light left at most. The rudiments of sailing were still unknown to him, but he did not want lessons and he could not wait. It was a small boat, a small sail; not enough moving parts to get too much wrong, he figured. Out he pushed over the shallows. He gripped the rigging. Wetted a finger in his mouth, raised it to meet the wind's direction. Felt a breeze. Hoisted his sail.

He expected nothing to happen, so he didn't let himself become dismayed. He knew it would take practice, knew he would have to learn. He unfurled the sail, swung the boom, lowered the centreboard, then strove to capture the wind's current in any way he could. After half an hour an invisible fist pushed into the sail's midriff, swelling it enough to pull the dinghy forward, and they were away, Ned and the boat, the boat and Ned, not fast, not thrill-inducing, but moving under power not their own: sailing. He fiddled with the rudder, which was functional but not entirely smooth, guiding them back and forth across the bay. Zigzagging, switchbacking, watching at all times the play of the wind in the body of the sail.

He wanted to fly out into the river proper, but as soon as he gained enough confidence the day betrayed him, the sun losing itself in the west. The final light died over the hills. He turned to the shore and sailed for home, the oars still stowed, a feeling of ecstatic accomplishment flashing through him, a feeling beyond language. His life widened. Time wobbled. He grazed the truth of his dreams, grazed a world frozen perfect, if only for the length of the dusk.

~

Over the next week it became clear to him how poor a sailor he was. He'd thought the processes would be intuitive, but they weren't. He didn't know the first thing about sailing, wasn't able to effectively operate the sail, didn't know what to do when the wind changed, or when the waves got up, or when he wanted to alter course, and when he did get the sail up he couldn't figure out how to get it working in unison with the rudder. The two things were constantly in conflict. He'd blow about on the river's face for hours, going nowhere.

And he loved it. He was hopeless on water, and he didn't care all that much. It was enough for him to be on those golden planks, free of soil, unmoored from the orchard and his family. And eventually, he started to get better. He adjusted the size and shape of the rudder so it sat more easily in the water, so it fought him less. He discovered how to make it talk to the sail, or at least listen to it. He learned how to read the mood of the weather in the movement of the eucalypts before he was loose and lost on the river. He figured out how to set the sail in order to snare the wind, and while he never caught all of it, it was usually enough to get the boat moving in the rough direction he desired. He learned how to react to a change in the breeze or current, how to tack windward, how to shift leeward. This rarely worked well: he spent a lot of time twisting about on the face of the river. And it was never long before he became stuck into the river's swirling centre, in the mess of whirlpools that grabbed the boat, shook it, strafed it, spat it out spinning.

In those whirlpooled moments he was powerless. But the boat did not mind—it sat high in the water, it bladed cleanly through the chop, it reacted to every yank of the current with a delicate counter-step—so neither did he. And once he was beyond the whirlpools they did not matter, their power was null. He forgot them. Was free to go wherever the wind and water would let him.

Jackbird often came with him, spouting his usual ideas and schemes as he sat in the middle of the boat, away from the water. On the river his bluster was even more exposed than on land, but Ned didn't mind. It was good to share the joy of his achievement. Good to have company. And Jackbird was smart—he helped Ned find the sandy depths good for catching flathead, helped him understand the changeability of the river quicker than Ned would've figured out on his own.

But Ned preferred to take Maggie. She gave no advice, requested no destination. She didn't compliment him on his acquisition of the sail, but that was all right. She just sat there as Ned sailed them in whatever direction he could manage or whatever way the wind chose, leaning over the side, leaning on the glowing Huon pine, carving furrows into the river with fingertips.

If they went north, towards the river mouth, they found bends and bays meeting paddocks that sloped down to the shore. The smoke of coastal villages hung in the air. White beaches called to Ned from both the physical world and his dreams. He noted the ones along the river, began planning nights he'd spend on their sands, nights where he'd watch fire spit green flames from salt-drenched driftwood.

If they went south the river was straighter, wider, revealing a bigger sky and more of the world. In the distance, mountains fudged the horizon. From his shining deck he could see the forest behind Telle's garden. See the shape of it in its entirety, matching the close-up sketches he'd made in his mind while walking through it. On the eastern side he saw another forest, one that mirrored the western one he knew. Similar trees and colours spread back from both banks. There was a symmetry to the contours of the land on each side; crests rose in synchronicity, and streams fed into the river from similar angles. It was as if the two forests had once been whole, and were forced apart by the coming of the saltwater. Although where the one behind Telle's ended in a belt of farmland, the eastern forest climbed a hill, then the foot of a low mountain, then dipped and spread across land beyond sight.

Ned pointed this out to Maggie, as well as the other things he saw: low-flying pelicans, gulls working at schools of baitfish, the treacherous currents he'd learned to avoid, a fur seal's dark flipper raised as if in greeting. At all of this she smiled and murmured encouragement, never withdrawing her fingers from the water.

Taking Maggie out on the river swelled Ned with the feeling of being useful, of being impressive. Of doing something worth talking about. With her in his boat the world seemed right, and better things felt inevitable. The summer would break. Rains would muddy the dust. The orchard would drip with healthy fruit, just as the requisitioning ended. The mare would gallop unhindered. Toby would come home bored and whole, and word would finally come from Bill. Their father would rise and be restitched into himself. All of it would happen: everything proper, everything good.

~

At the end of his first week of sailing he found his father burning sheets of newspaper outside the house. They weren't meant to be lighting fires. There was a ban: the temperatures, the lack of rain. A stray spark could lick the valley into hell. Yet flames tongued William West's boots, snarling through newsprint.

Ned didn't ask his father why he was doing it. He knew what was in the cindered pages. The reports remained hollow. The absence was now so vast that Ned couldn't think about it. He could only remain upright by thinking of Bill the way he had as a child: Bill uncannily competent, Bill near to invincible.

Eventually his father noticed Ned on the other side of the smoke. Looked at his son for a while, then gestured at his chest, his mouth. 'They taught me this. Calms you down, when things aren't looking too flash.'

Ned hadn't realised his father was doing the slow breathing again. He'd been too focused on the fire. Now he heard the air pausing in his father's chest, before running in a steady stream out his nose.

'No doubt they taught your brothers too.' He balled another sheet of paper in his hand. Fed it to the flames. 'It helps.'

Ned didn't know what to say. His father talking about breathing, talking about his brothers: it brought back the night Bill had come home after helping his friend rescue the ram.

How in the driveway he'd fallen out of the truck, exhausted and unspeaking. And how before he'd made it inside, as Ned and Toby had watched from the window, their father had gone out to meet him. Ned was sure the old man was going to belt Bill, or at least grab him by the ear. But instead, their father had only stood before him, doing this breathing thing, shaking as he did it. Shaking all over, shaking hard enough to fall. Before he did, Bill caught his elbow. Snatched it from the air and propped the old man up. Looked into his face and copied the slow, deep breaths until their chests were mirrors of movement, pumping and collapsing with measured synchronicity. If they'd spoken, Ned hadn't seen it.

Remembering this tightened him up. It was a vice on his neck, a belt around his throat, so he began talking about the boat, about how he'd got a sail, how he'd rigged it up, how he'd caught some decent-sized flathead just that afternoon. How he'd taken Maggie out, how he thought she enjoyed it. How easily the boat handled the river, like a falcon in flight, like a Russian dancer. As if it had not been sawn and built but had grown out of the river itself, massaged into shape by the water's touch.

A look swam onto his father's face. A memory arriving. 'Some fellas in town asked me about that boat.' He rubbed the smoke off his eyes. 'Looks like you found a real treasure.'

Ned remembered Singline. The oddness of the interaction. 'I've been lucky.'

His father grunted. 'How's that tiger cat, then?'

'Getting there.' Ned said it flatly, but it was a deflection. He'd fed the quoll an hour earlier. When he'd opened the lid of the crate it had flown up to his hand in a liquid flash, snatching the egg from his grasp before he could react. Before he could stop its claws flaring open the plush skin on the inside of his wrist. It took the egg into the crate and devoured it in seconds, cracking and slurping.

Afterwards it had rolled onto its back, yawned open the armoury of its jaw and stretched out its limbs, showing Ned the ease of its strength. Showing him the place on its rear leg where it had torn off the bandage. Showing him a neat pink scar, edged by snowy fur.

~

A still dawn. Perhaps not enough wind to get it done, even though it had to be done. Ned lay in bed, hearing stillness out his window, imagining not doing it. Imagining arguments and strategies to avoid it. It was reasonable, he thought; he could make it work. But the longer he lay there, the clearer that version of himself became in his mind. A wheedling, avoiding, rationalising Ned. Changing rules, fleeing problems. The sort of person his father had no time for. He thought long and hard about that. Then he was up, dressed and out the door.

At the waterline he met Callie, her arm still strapped. In her free hand she held the note he'd slid through her window the night before.

'What's all this about?'

In the note he'd asked her to meet him. Hadn't given a reason why. Now he hefted the crate under his arm. 'No putting this off. Thought you might want to be there.'

Callie took in the crate. Lost the tension in her expression. 'Where?'

159

Ned pointed to the eastern bank. 'Over there.'

She followed his arm, then looked at her own injured one. At the crate. 'Are you as stupid as my brother?'

'It's possible.'

He put the crate in the centre of the dinghy and laid a heavy blanket on top of it. Then he pushed the boat over the runners into the shallows. He offered to help Callie climb in but she did it without him, awkwardly. Ned pushed off and jumped in over the transom.

There was not enough wind to make it worth sailing, so he rowed them down the shoreline, heading south. Once they reached Telle's place he turned into the river. The quoll needed dense, high trees in which to hunt birds. It needed valleys and heights where farmers didn't set traps or aim rifles. It needed a forest, and the only one he knew where it might be safe was the eastern partner of the one behind Telle's garden.

Away from land a breeze became discernible. He got the sail up, tacked into the wind and found a way to zag east. It was slow going, but they were not in a rush, not now that they had got away without being questioned or followed. Callie sat near the crate. Ned focused on the tiller, the boom, the sail. Let the physicality of the task chase away his hesitations.

When the sun's full shape was in the sky they coasted into the shallows. Heat was already building. They jumped out, and Ned began pulling the boat onto a pebbly beach, taking care not to run the wood over any large or sharp rocks. When it was above the tideline he retrieved the crate. Behind them was a wall of pale paperbarks, scrubby ferns threading around the trunks. Callie walked into them. Ned followed, holding the crate close to his chest.

The paperbarks shared the land with she-oaks, whose fallen needles smothered other vegetation and formed dry glades. There was no path to follow, so they moved from glade to glade. After half an hour Callie turned to him.

'Here?'

Ned shook his head. 'Need bigger trees.' He pointed through the she-oaks to the little mountain in the distance. It was covered by greener textures, taller trunks. She adjusted her sling. They kept going.

The walking got easier when they found a stream. They could drink from it, and because the vegetation was scrubbier on its banks they could walk beside it, following its path into the heights. Clear water rolled over brown-black stones. The trees were now mostly eucalypts, blue gums and white gums and stringybarks and, most notably to Ned, black gums: prime quoll habitat. He'd read that in an old field guide that had belonged to his mother. But he still felt uneasy; if he turned around he could see the river behind him, the boats it held, the people on their decks. Farmland still felt close too, even though he couldn't see any paddocks. There was an emptiness to the horizon, a feeling of cultivation.

It wasn't until they'd ascended a damp slope, where the black gums began mingling with myrtles, that he felt surer. Here the trees were taller, wetter. Moss crawled over the trunks and raised roots of the myrtles. He stopped. Put the crate on the ground.

Callie was at his shoulder. 'Here?'

'I suppose so.' He looked up at the canopy. High branches,

thick foliage, small gaps of green-stained light. He avoided the rumbling growls he could hear at his feet and the sudden rattling of the crate, as if the quoll had read his intentions from inside the box.

'Do you want to do it?'

He hoped she'd say yes, but she shook her head. For a moment he waited, not for anything to happen but for a feeling to come over him, something that told him he was ready, that he was doing the right thing. No such feeling came; he felt only a lack of rhythm in his pulse and breathing, and rising nausea. Before it could bubble out of him, he ripped off the crate's lid.

The quoll came out fast, all muscle and colour. No suspicion, no trepidation. A vigorous leap onto the moss and loam, its nose twitching at all the cleanness. Paws padding at the dirt, tail ruddering left and right. It turned to Ned, nose still working at the air. Expecting food. When he offered it none, when he did nothing but stare and grip his breath and clench his jaw, it turned to the nearest tree. It leaped onto the trunk and began climbing, fast and assured, laddering up the bark with natural authority. The spots on its pelt shone against the wood like a patterned moth, a living quilt.

At the first branch the quoll paused, sniffed. Opened its mouth, showed its fangs. Ned felt Callie beside him, whispering something he couldn't hear. He couldn't hear anything. He wasn't breathing. The quoll closed its jaw and turned back to the trunk. It blinked up the tree, into the higher limbs and denser foliage. Ned rubbed at the heat flooding his eyes. When he removed his fingers, the quoll was gone.

# 17

NED DIDN'T TALK about the quoll often in the years that followed. He didn't grow into much of a storyteller, and when there were opportunities to bring up the subject, he chose not to. When it came to him while he was snorkelling, as the leather-jacket tried to skewer his palm, he couldn't find a way to convert the experience into meaningful language. At other times when he remembered the quoll, he worried that the men around him wouldn't understand. While working on the mainland, where quolls had nearly been exterminated, the rouseabouts would have asked why he hadn't killed it. The loggers toppling the White Knights would have flung wet bottles at his head. The saltwater stock workers would have just stared. The men he hired on his orchard would have wondered why their employer was wasting their time with childish recollections. It was only Callie whom he could speak to about the quoll. Only she had known the touch of its company. Nobody else could come at it.

But then there were his daughters. Sharp little whips of

children he could hardly believe were his. He didn't say a lot to them; the way they whirled about his life didn't leave much room for comment. But he did what he could, what he knew how to do, and he didn't deny them much, which wasn't as hard as it might have been—after his trip to Britain his orchard had done well, and the family was comfortable. The new variety of spray had allowed his apples to thrive, had meant his crops were larger, the yields more predictable. A marvellous invention—a poison that filled his trees with life. Other orchardists in the valley, the ones who hadn't bought in to the spray, had given up. Thousands of apple trees had been wrenched out and replaced with vines. People wanted wine at the table these days. Ned remained happy with beer. The odd brandy, if the situation called for it.

When Sally was twelve, Grace eleven and Harriet seven, they found a kitten in a knot of blackberries: a tawny, skittish thing. Ned had no time for cats, but he tolerated it. When they asked him to let it in the house, he usually did. When they asked him to buy it food, he did. When their mother had gone to see a doctor in Launceston—she'd torn a muscle in her chest while carrying in the washing—and they wanted him to bring the cat to school when he picked them up, he did.

He'd known it was a foolish idea while wrestling the cat into the truck, claws snagging on his forearms, in the webbing of his fingers. His conviction grew even stronger when the cat, anxious and mad in the flying prison of the truck, climbed onto his headrest and pissed down his neck. By the time he was at the school gates he was a figure of bleeding, stinking rage, and all he could say to his frightened daughters—they'd never seen him lose his temper before—was that the bloody cat had to go; it was a menace, a terror; it was harder to control than the quoll he'd once had, and that had been a proper animal, proper wild.

On the way back to the orchard, the cat now stretched across their laps, his girls began to relax. They stroked at its shivers. They sniffed the acrid air. They asked him: What quoll? Quolls aren't pets, Dad.

So he spooled out his relationship with the quoll, from the moment he found it in his trap. He told them how their Aunt Maggie had been worried about her chickens, at a time they couldn't afford to lose even an egg. How he'd been tempted to kill it. How he perhaps should have, but instead had herded it back to health. He told them of Telle the vet, of her garden and forest. Of keeping the quoll secret, of its gradual recovery, of the paint-like glossiness it gained from feasting on duck eggs. Of the speed and power that flashed unpredictably from its body. Of taking it across the river. Of watching it disappear into high myrtle-shadow.

As Ned told the story, the quoll came back to him. It had long felt like a memory from another life, but now he could again see its red-purple wound, its snapping jaw, its quicksilver movements. Its pink, corrugated footpads. Its brilliant coat. Its fierce presence, filling that summer with a kind of primeval purpose. He suddenly felt very old. Felt the distance between his youth and what he was now. He flexed his wrists, touched his face. Wondered if the troubled boy of that summer would recognise the man he'd become.

His girls, usually inclined to peel away from him the moment they got home, kept up with questions. Did the quoll try to escape? Did it bite him? How big was it? Did he ever see it again? Around the kitchen they went. Around the garden their mother had planted out the back, afternoon light rubbing off a towering wattle. He tried to answer but he'd spent all his emotion in the truck, and he couldn't get the details of the story straight, or the order of events. Had it bitten him? It must have. Had his father known about it before or after they built the boatshed? Had its leg healed cleanly, as he'd always believed, or would a limp have been inevitable? Now that he was talking about it, he realised that his recollections might not be as clear as he'd assumed.

It was a horrible sensation, feeling that the facts of his life had blurred. He wondered if his past was slipping away, easy as a quoll into a myrtle. He was glad when his wife got home. Glad her presence would distract their daughters, glad normalcy could return to the house. But when she came into the kitchen she gave him a tight smile and he saw how forced her face was, and the tired slump to her shoulders, and the gladness left him.

The girls swarmed her, demanding attention, not knowing why she'd had to go to the city. Dad says he had a pet quoll, they told her. Is it true? Did he ever tell you? Is he making it up?

'Is that so?' She took a plate of food from Ned, and throughout dinner she asked their children the usual questions about school, about their days. Open questions for stubborn Sally, direct ones for quiet Grace. Deflecting the task of talking onto the children. Ned could see the falseness in her expressions, the energy it was costing her to stay sound. After eating, the girls went to their rooms. Ned found a bottle of brandy. Plinked out the cork.

'Not the washing, then?'

His wife took the chipped crystal tumbler from his hand. 'No.' Tossed its heat down her throat. 'Not in that way.'

It wasn't a torn muscle, she said. Nothing strained or overworked. She told him how the doctor had questioned her, examined her, felt for lumps and irregularities, listened to her breathing and heart rate, and could find nothing that explained the ache in her chest. Or anything that accounted for the rattle in her throat and her shortness of breath, which she hadn't mentioned to Ned because she hadn't wanted to worry him. The doctor had taken her pulse again, this time from her wrist. He'd turned her hand over in his. Felt at a sticky residue on her palm.

'What's this?' he'd asked.

She'd told him it was the same stuff that was always there on washing days: the spray Ned and his men used on the orchard, wafting over the apples, settling on the bedding she wouldn't have hung out if they'd remembered to tell her they were going to do it. Settling on tea towels, on shirts, on her skin and in her pores. The chemical taste of it in her mouth, coating her tongue, clogging her nostrils. A thick film of it on her hands from dragging all those spoiled sheets and clothes off the line. Not coming off as she did all the washing again, no matter how many loads were required.

Ned had begun to breathe very fast. His hand hurt. He looked down and saw that he was squeezing his fingers, twisting the knuckles against his grip. His face was hot and his throat itched. He thought of all the times he'd sprayed his trees. Thought of the thick gloves he wore when he did it, the strips

167

of old flannel shirt that he wrapped around his mouth and nose. Of his heavy clouds of death, wafting over the orchard. He asked what else the doctor had said, and his wife told him that she'd been booked in with four specialists. The appointments began next week.

They were quiet for a while. Ned knew he should say something comforting, something reassuring, but he couldn't make it happen. His mind had been tugged apart and he couldn't concentrate. The doctor was a quack, he thought, and everything would be fine; these specialists would sort things out, it was probably just one of those infections, nobody was tougher than his wife, everyone knew that, everyone in the whole valley—someone should tell that idiot doctor, this soft doctor who clearly didn't know what people who didn't live in cities were made of.

He was still wrenching at his knuckles. A rough snort blew out his nose. He realised he was still breathing too fast. That the air was coming in and out of him all wrong. His wife had put a hand on his arm, and when that didn't slow him down, she embraced him. I should be holding you, he wanted to say: I should be holding you. Even though there was surely nothing wrong with her.

When he had stilled she let him go, swallowed some brandy and coughed. A normal cough, not one that sounded particularly hard or wet, but it was enough to make Ned reach again for the bottle. Poured more brandy, tried to talk once more. Failed again. His words still stumbling over each other, none finding a way past the wall of panic within him, a rising wall, a wall of blades.

But he wasn't the only one who'd heard the cough. Harriet stumbled back into the kitchen, tears smudging her face. At first Ned thought she'd heard what his wife had said, had somehow understood what it meant. But it was only that she couldn't sleep, she told them. She couldn't stop thinking about the scary animal that Dad was hiding under the house. The scary wild animal. It was going to get her—it was going to eat her.

Callie coughed again. Looked at Ned. An old warmth in her eyes, far-off but unfaded. Tempered by her stiff strength. She pulled their daughter into her lap and stroked the child's hair, telling her no, there was no scary animal under the house. It had been gone for a long, long time. And it hadn't been scary at all: it was just a cute quoll, a friendly little fellow that her dad had looked after, and when it was feeling better they'd taken home to its family. Wasn't that nice? Home to its family. Up in the lovely green trees.

# 18

*Ned,*

*Well, that's that. You've probably seen it in the paper. I imagine the reports aren't giving much away, but trust you me: the fat lady's singing and she's got a loudspeaker.*

*Biggest thing I shot at this whole time was a pelican. Most danger I was in was from the rations. But I suppose it is good to be alive and to remain handsome.*

*You still won't be seeing me anytime soon. Apparently there'll be an occupation force, made up of men like yours truly. Last in, last out—you know how it goes. Although I guess you don't. Neither do I, come to think of it.*

*And if you think I'm coming back to watch apples grow after that, then you're dead wrong. I've been talking to these fellows from New South Wales and Queensland, and I've decided that I'm going to give it a red hot go over there. I'll be a jackaroo, or if I can't swing that, a rouseabout. You can work your way all over the country on the sheep's back. I'm going*

*to start south and head all the way up to Longreach. I'll go to*
*every station that'll have me.*

*Don't worry. I'll come back to the orchard eventually.*
*Bill's going to need somebody to boss about. When you see*
*him, tell him he and Dad will have to do without me for a*
*while. He'll be over the moon, no doubt.*
*Toby*

~

The letter had come the day after they'd released the quoll. Ned
read his brother's words twice, five times, ten. He felt drenched
by the images they brought him. Toby staring over hot, flat seas.
Toby strolling through foreign cities, pointing a gun at fearful
strangers. Toby on horseback, herding cattle; Toby clipping
fleece off wriggling sheep. Toby carving a life in the mainland's
dust and dirt.

He only stopped reading when he heard knuckles rapping
the front door. He left the letter unfolded on the kitchen table,
next to the papers, where his father and Maggie wouldn't be
able to miss it.

It was Telle. Behind her was the mare, tethered to a post.
It took Ned a few seconds to take them both in, to understand
what was happening. He'd never seen Telle anywhere but at
her place, where she seemed to fit better. Here on the orchard
she was taller, harder. Had brittled herself against the unbroken
light of the land outside her garden. Her trousers were clean,
and her flannel shirt looked ironed. She had her arms crossed.
Was looking him in the eye.

'She's all sorted.' A nod at the mare, then her eyes were
back on his. 'Hadn't seen you in a while, and I was headed this

way anyway. Thought I'd drop her off.'

Ned dipped his eyes. He hadn't been going to Telle's as much as he should have been. He'd meant to, but lately there had been too many mornings that held soft winds, irresistible winds, and he'd hurtled riverward, telling himself that he'd go trapping and shooting at Telle's the following day, only to wake up the next morning and find himself again unable to do anything but sail.

'Sorry. I'll be back tomorrow.' Even as he said it, even as he knew it was the right thing to say and do, he regretted it. Over the recent mornings he'd become more confident in his skills, more assured. In the favourable conditions the boat had glided over the water like a limber skater, responding to his touch with an intuition of its own. Knowledge leaping from the wood. He'd begun plotting a longer trip, an overnight voyage that would take him past daggered reefs, past heads, past the last whirlpool. One that took him somewhere he could view a flat horizon. Somewhere he hadn't been in a decade: the river mouth.

'No need.' Telle gave him a forgiving smile. 'Haven't seen a rabbit in days. I think they've had it. Seems like the ones you didn't account for were taken by this heat.'

'I must still owe you.'

A small shake of her head. 'Best tomato crop I've ever had. Debt's settled.' She shifted her eyes to where the land sloped and dipped. 'Although I wouldn't mind having a look at this boat I keep hearing about.'

~

Telle wasn't the only one who wanted to see the boat. A steady stream of people had been coming to Limberlost for over a week. At first Ned had been confused—how did they know about it? Who had told them? When Jackbird revealed that he may have mentioned the boat to one or two people, which Ned knew really meant ten or twelve, his confusion shifted to anger. Not at Jackbird—Ned knew his tongue could not be trained or halted—but at the attention. The boat was his, nobody else's business, something for himself and his sister. For his father, if the old man ever wished it. For his brothers.

But when the men and women of the valley came down the driveway, wanting a glimpse, he found that he couldn't deny them. Part of it was manners, but a greater part was pride. He saw the way they looked at him after he led them to the shoreline and revealed his green-gold treasure—like he'd been plunged in molten minerals and recast in a new skin. With their eyes on him he told them where he'd got the boat, crediting Falmouth, crediting luck. He'd dip a finger in the olive dust that still lined the boatshed floor, and tell them how he'd scoured the paint off. Told them of the shellac he'd dabbed over the holes, of the rudder he'd coaxed out of oak, of the sail he'd bought from Singline. He invited them to smell the timber, and feasted on their reactions as their noses caught the wood's spice. If the weather was good, he pushed the boat out into the river, showing them how easily it cut through the water. If there were children, he took them with him. Held the tiller as they waved at their parents on the shore.

As well as families and groups of friends there came men on their own—men claiming knowledge and experience. Sailors and shipwrights who wanted to chew over the boat's quality. They had seen grander vessels, they were all quick to tell him. Wondrous creations down south, yachts and ketches of design and beauty that defied natural order, the sight of which made grown adults shake. But Ned noticed that each of these wise, gruff, all-knowing men could not leave without laying a palm on the boat's golden timber. Could not walk away without a final stare.

It was with these men that Ned's pride flared hottest, when he felt his achievement with the boat had run beyond his dreams. He began to think he'd done something remarkable. He started to wonder if he had an eye for things that others didn't. This sensation was heightened when one of the men—the only one who didn't claim to be an expert—asked if he could return with someone else. This curious man was small, middle-aged, perhaps the same age as Ned's father, but more assured and much smarter dressed. His neat suit lent him a sharpened look, and the perfect ovals of his gold-rimmed glasses gave him an aura of intelligence and money. When he leaned in to sniff at the wood, his face glowed with energy.

'Marvellous, young man. Absolutely marvellous. I don't know a lot about watercraft, but boy am I developing an interest. I wonder: would you mind if I popped back with a friend of mine? He knows a thing or two about wood and wind and whatnot. I'd love to hear his opinion on this little gem of yours.'

Ned felt himself lifting, swelling. Felt a specialness claiming him that he had not sought. He nodded, shook the man's hand and watched him pick his way through the bracken back to the orchard, a clever smile on his thin lips.

These pulses of pride never lasted long. Ned wasn't shaped to be impressed by himself. Once the visitors were gone he pivoted away from his self-regard and back to the river. And of all the adults he took to see his boat, the reaction he enjoyed most was Telle's. She, of all people other than perhaps his father, knew the effort he'd put into obtaining it. So when she saw it and slowly raised an eyebrow, slowly drew on an impressed smile, Ned felt not pride but something simpler. A particular kind of happiness: the kind that felt earned.

He told her the story of it, his words coming faster than with the others, without artifice or caution. Told her how he'd known there was something wonderful under the old paint from the moment he saw it lying on Falmouth's dirt. How the boat had spoken to him, guided him. How when he sailed it, he felt like a fuller version of himself. How he and Callie had used it to take the quoll to the forest on the eastern shore.

Telle smiled. 'Leg healed up all right, then?'

Ned remembered it darting into the green-dark canopy. 'Yes, indeed.' He grasped at the memory and found a chasm within him, ringing with echoes of teeth, of blood.

'Well. That's something.' She knocked a fist on the boat's hull. 'And so's this.'

They walked back to the road. Telle looked over at the rows of apple trees. 'Tell your father I said hello.' She kept walking, not slowing down. 'Tell him he's not friendless.'

~

Days of sailing, nights of planning. Ned's trip to the river mouth began to solidify. For a while he thought he'd take Jackbird, but soon realised he didn't want company, that the journey required solitude. He decided that on the day of the trip he'd leave in the morning and make for one of the sheltered white beaches he'd glimpsed in the northern bends. There he'd build a shelter and spend the afternoon exploring the nearby clearings and forests, taking in the fauna, the topography. He'd catch fish in the river, and at night he'd cook their white-flaking flesh over a fire that he'd also sleep next to, under the bright-scattered stars, in a swag that had once belonged to Bill. He'd rise at dawn, get straight in the boat and keep sailing north until he reached the river's end.

Once there, he'd hover on the broad border of estuary and ocean. He'd become acquainted with the bar, the tide, the currents. He'd eat cold fish from the night before, try to snare a squid from a weedy reef. He'd float, drift, tack. And he'd look for the place he'd gone ten years earlier. He'd find the exact spot where the mad whale had erupted. He'd see it and know it and feel it, instantly, as certain as sunrise.

He'd stare at that field of water until all the things he could not handle were rinsed out of him, and all that remained within him was the memory of that night: the whale, the warmth of the coat, his brothers, his father, the starlight. Afterwards, he'd turn around and sail for home, which would take the rest of the day, probably some of the evening. With luck, he'd make it back to Limberlost before it was completely dark.

~

He was eager to get going. But the next day he woke to the first overcast morning in weeks. Clouds were thick in the sky, pale above the river yet dark on the horizon: premonitions of a summer storm. He put off the trip and helped his father in the orchard instead.

At midday, as they were eating lunch on the porch, a car came down the driveway. Two men got out. More curious townies, Ned thought. He was relieved to see them: an excuse to get out of work. He put down his sandwich and walked over to them.

'Boatshed's this way.' He turned to the river, kept walking. Stopped when he realised they weren't following him. He looked again. Saw that they were wearing jackets, and that one was carrying a cracked leather briefcase. They regarded him with confusion, then moved towards the porch, where his father had stood up, was brushing crumbs from his knees, straightening his hat.

'Better go see to the last row of Coxes,' he called to Ned.

Ned lingered. Watched the men wait, unsuited to the dry dirt, but patient. Two creased forms of patience.

'Not a question, lad.' His father's voice, hard as chipped stone. Shoving him back into the orchard.

By the end of the afternoon he'd checked every branch. Had bent and searched every fruit for blemishes, rot, black spot and codling moth. Sweat plastered his body. It was tiring work, more work than usual, because the crop was strong. One of the strongest he could remember. He hoped that the men from the bank had noticed it. He hoped they'd been able to see the red-yellow glint of thousands of robust apples from the farmhouse. Had seen that most were the size of boxers' fists. The obvious wealth in all that life. He hoped they'd accounted for it, and had left reassured.

But when he came in for dinner, they were still there. And there they remained as he washed off the day, as he thumbed the dirt off the potatoes, as he rationed tiny flecks of butter into the mash. His father still on the porch with them. All three talking quietly. The scribble of pencils louder than any voice.

~

Ned didn't see Maggie until after dinner, after the bankers had left, after his father had drifted inside and gone straight to bed. She came in late, dirt on her clothes, dust in her hair. She moved stiffly, but pink heat glowed through the muck on her face. She looked alive, renewed. Ned did not need to ask to know that she'd been riding the mare.

He warmed some milk on the stove. 'How was she?'

'Bit cautious, bit slow. But steady. Healthy.' Maggie ripped a hard corner of bread from an old loaf. 'Thanks to old Telle.'

Ned stirred the milk.

Maggie worked her teeth through the crust. 'And you.'

He felt his breath release, his shoulders unkink. Maggie was grinning through a mouthful of stale crumbs. He didn't know what to say. There weren't words that could fit his relief, his gratitude, his hot stab of love, so he just nodded. When the milk bubbled he switched off the stove and poured it into a mug for her.

'Did you read Toby's letter?'

'The one you artfully left on the table for public consumption?' Her grin fading. 'Yes. Looks like it'll be a while until we see him again.'

'He'll come back, though. He said he would.'

She blew at the milk. Her breath rippled its floating skin. 'As long as he can stay out of trouble.'

'Did Dad read it?'

'One would assume.'

'So he knows Toby's all right.'

She took a sip. Exhaled. 'Yes, Ned. We all know Toby's all right.'

~

Later, Ned lay in bed waiting for the storm to break above them, for hard rain to attack the roof. But the sky stayed dry and silent. In the morning the clouds were still there, not having moved, or if they had, having changed shape and structure and colour in a way that mirrored the previous day's ominousness. He considered beginning his trip to the mouth, but couldn't go through with it, not with the sky the way it was.

Instead he tinkered with the boat, checked the sail, checked his fishing lines, checked the bite and snag of his hooks. Only two visitors came that day: the sharp little man who'd asked if he could return, and the associate he'd mentioned, a nondescript man in humbler clothes than the suited gentleman. A man much like the sailors and shipwrights who'd come before, but not carrying the ego and self-importance they had. He could have been any one of the hundreds of farmers, labourers and rivermen in the valley. The one thing he wasn't, Ned was sure of, was the suited man's friend, despite what the gentleman had said. There was a deference, a stiltedness to their interactions. It was a relationship between an employer and employee, at best. Ned could read it when he saw them coming down to the boatshed. Could tell that things weren't as the suited man had presented them to him.

The suited man greeted Ned warmly, as if they were old companions. 'Master West, what an honour it is to be back here. Thank you for allowing me to bring along my old chum Harry. He advises me on all things to do with watercraft. Awfully clever chap. Knows his way around rudders and sails like no one else. Isn't that right, Harry?'

The man named Harry ignored his introducer. He'd already moved to the shed and was circling the boat. Marching slow eyes across it. He put his hands on it, knelt down, bent over. He breathed in its scent. He lay on his back, stroked its angles. He leaned in and fiddled with the centreboard. Shook at the mast. He frowned at the rudder, but otherwise did not let emotion touch his features. After he'd seen and touched and tasted every part of the boat he directed a few short questions at Ned. Where did he get it? Did he know how it came into Falmouth's possession? What had he treated the timber with? Had he sailed it much? Did it leak? Had he interfered with the structure at all?

Ned didn't like the way this man spoke without looking at him, but he still gave him the truth. When he was satisfied, Harry left the boatshed, walked to the shore. Gave the gentleman a single nod as he passed him.

The man's face squirmed. He drew in a long breath. Pushed it out through his nose, spread his hands, showed his teeth.

'Now here's the thing, Master West. You're a smart young man, so you've no doubt cottoned on to my intentions. But I shall say it plainly, so there is no confusion, and so that you do not feel misled: I'd very much like to acquire this boat of yours.'

Ned tried to make his face polite. 'Thank you for your interest, sir. But it's not for sale.'

The gentleman laughed. 'Of course it's not. These things are never for sale, are they? Until they're sold.' He removed his glasses. Fogged them with his breath, rubbed them with a handkerchief he pulled from his jacket. 'You are aware of this boat's properties, I take it?'

'Huon pine. Sails nicely. As I said: it's not for sale.'

'Yes, Huon pine. They made quite a few of them. But not many like this. Not many at all, did they, Harry?' Harry, now standing nearby, shook his head.

'And of the ones they did make, many have been lost or destroyed. People have been looking for a boat like this for a long time. People like me.'

Ned couldn't see a way of making them leave without being rude.

The gentleman stepped towards him. 'I am prepared to pay you top price, Master West. The absolute height of what this boat could be considered to be worth.'

'I appreciate your interest, sir, but—'

The gentleman cut him off. 'This war, lad. It's tough on everyone. Tough in so many ways.' He said the words like they meant something else. 'Think beyond yourself for a moment. Think of more than your appetite for sailing. Imagine what that money could do. Imagine what it could mean.' He pulled on a soft smile: teacherly, grandfatherly. Turned to the orchard. Returned his glasses to his face and peered at the apple trees.

Ned pushed his heels into the pebbles, searching for the steadiness that had fled him. 'Good crop coming in. Don't need money.'

'A bumper crop, my boy. One to be proud of. But a crop that is still a few long weeks from harvest.' The gentleman raised a palm. 'Please, scrub that comment from your mind. I am not here to pressure you, or to make observations and implications.

I want only to impress upon you the great opportunity of my offer. I will reiterate: the highest conceivable value.'

He named his price. Let it hang and expand in the air. He clasped his hands together, closed his damp lips, and waited. Harry hovered on the shore beyond him, hands in his pockets.

After a minute, Ned gave his final answer. The only one he could live with.

~

The next morning the clouds were gone and the summer scorched back to life. Ned did not hesitate. He was on the water twenty minutes after waking.

The wind was light but it was at his back, so he did not have to row or struggle to work the boat forward. In an hour he was further north than he'd ever sailed before, the slate-blue water carrying him with ease. White clouds were soft and mountainous in the sky. Gulls dived into schools of baitfish, which were hunted from below by the slippery figures of black-back salmon. By mid-morning the river doglegged west and widened into a large estuary.

Ned began looking for a suitable camping site, but every beach he saw was too close to towns, jetties, shacks, pilot lights. When the river narrowed again the beaches were small, lumpy and exposed. For half an hour he worried that he'd got it all wrong, that there'd be nowhere for him to create the camp he'd imagined. But he kept looking and soon saw, on the banks of an inlet that ran back from the river's course, a stand of tall trees. He tacked towards them, and when he rounded a small head he came upon a cove that hadn't been visible from the river's centre. The shadows of the trees were darkening the water. At their roots was a beach of pale, untrodden sand.

He coasted into the cove, to the shore. Took down the sail, leaped into the shallows and hauled the boat up. He walked the length of the beach, looking for markers of ownership. Found only trees, scrub and orange-ochred rocks. No tracks, no fences, no signs promising bullets for interlopers. The sand was soft and uncompacted, swallowing his boots at every step.

A settling shiver trickled down Ned's skin. He made sure all his gear was secure under the boat's seat, then began exploring the forest. For a few hours he stepped through the trees, winding among paperbarks and black gums and the ubiquitous coastal she-oaks. Walked off all the thoughts that came to him. Walked himself empty.

When he'd roamed all the wild land available to him, when he'd mapped the contours of it into his mind—something he found strangely satisfying, as if knowledge of this place was a possession that could enrich him—he returned to the beach's softness. With the sun lowering, he pushed the boat back out but only into the little cove, looking for sandflats. With his handline he caught three flathead, which he filleted back on the shore. He corralled some river stones into a circle and filled it with strips of curling paperbark and a few handfuls of she-oak needles. He struck a match, tossed it in. When the flames bit he poked in twigs, sticks, driftwood, and when coals formed he cooked his fillets on a flat rock he pushed into the orange heat.

By the time he'd finished eating it was dark. He washed his hands and face in the river and crawled into Bill's swag. Lay down between the fire and the boat. Watched green flames shudder up from salted driftwood. Fought everything out of his mind except the heat of the fire, the shadows of the trees, the pattern of the stars and the mouth of the river, and what it would mean, what it would feel like to be there again, what it would do for him.

~

In the morning the storm clouds were back, darker than before, dark as road tar. With them were gusting winds. They were what woke him: not dawn, as he'd planned, but a ragged nor'-wester, tearing up the sand and harassing the little forest. He stumbled to the head of the cove, still groggy with sleep, hoping to see a faultless sky on the horizon. Instead he saw a white-slashed river, foaming all the way to the mouth.

There was no choice to make. No course to take but the hard route home.

The conditions were even rougher than they looked from the shore, far rougher than anything he'd experienced before. The moment he left the cove the nor'-wester hit him hard, throwing the boat off course, knocking it against the waves. It took all of Ned's strength and skill to wrangle his way back down the river. He was constantly tacking back, pulling out his oars, fighting the savage gusts and the heeling of the boat. If he knew more about sailing he might have coped better. At no point did he feel in control, not for the whole trip. Wind cut him; water slapped him. His arms and back were wrenched by the work. They rang with pain, but he could not stop. At midday he ran out of fresh water. A deep throb hammered his skull. The weather did not relent. The only benefit to this frantic battle was that it gave him no time to dwell on the failure of the trip.

He limped into the bay at Limberlost late in the afternoon. He was crusted with salt, slick with sweat and spray. Half-asleep with exhaustion. Numb from toenail to eyelash. The glow within him splashed still and smokeless.

~

The fullness of the storm arrived that night. The pace of the wind increased with the darkness, racing down the valley, knifing through the trees. Gums creaked; pines swished. A deep and mournful whistle heralded each gust. Rain finally plummeted groundward: hours of ceaseless, heavy pelting, viscous as honey.

In the morning Ned and his father went to the orchard and found apples blanketing the ground. Hundreds. Thousands. Vibrant orbs shining on the already greening grass. They began gathering them up, not saying much. Ned knew there was a possibility that some of the less-damaged fruit could be sold to the cannery, but most of the fallen apples were unredeemable: their flesh bruised, their skin torn. They dropped them into canvas bags and carried them to the apple shed.

A suffocating dejectedness pressed on them. Ned found it hard to look at any part of the orchard without wanting to lie down or shout. He was still tired from his struggles on the river the previous day. Moisture had crawled through his boots. It all left him ragged and weary, so when he heard a sputtering growl, it took him a while to realise that it was an engine. His father was collecting apples from the far end of the orchard, and hadn't reacted. Ned put down his bucket and moved towards the sound.

He soon found its source: a truck, reversing down the lowest paddock, backing a trailer to the river. It was crunching over scrub, flattening bracken, snapping saplings. Ned began running. It wasn't meant to happen like this. As he ran he saw Maggie, riding the mare. She must have seen the truck, but she was galloping away from it, towards the house. Ned hoped she would go inside and stay there.

When he reached the shoreline the gentleman had manoeuvred his vehicle against the boatshed at an uneven angle. He had removed his jacket, lowered the trailer, and was in the process of shoving the boat onto it. He had the bow up, but couldn't seem to shift it any further. He put his back to the stern, bent his legs. A hoarse panting blew out of his mouth. As he began to heave, Ned reached him.

'Sir...'

He stumbled around, let the boat slip. 'Young West! In the nick of time.' His face was red and wet, his shirt drenched around the neck and armpits. A thick smell lifted from him: a sharp fume, obscuring the play of Huon pine in the air.

'Where's Harry?'

'Who? Oh.' The gentleman rubbed a sleeve at his forehead. 'Useless bastard. Don't need him, anyway, do we?'

He resumed his position at the stern and gestured for Ned to join him. Ned saw the splintered marks the gentleman had already gouged into the woodwork. Saw the shake in his legs, the fog in his eyes.

The man's face was all capillaries and sweat. He gestured at Ned. 'Come on, come on.'

Ned was about to move forward, or he wasn't—he didn't know; he felt sick—when he heard footsteps. He turned and saw his father marching over the flattened ferns. The old man strode past Ned, straight to the trailer. The gentleman only noticed him when he was a few feet away. He straightened. Fiddled at his shirt. Offered a hand.

'Ah, the father. What a...'

Then he was on the ground, on his back, William West standing over him, tall and grim. His fury everywhere.

'Thirty seconds to explain yourself.'

The gentleman wheezed. The wind had been knocked out of him. He squinted, scrabbled, tried to speak. Couldn't get anything out.

'It's his, Dad. I sold it to him.'

Ned's father turned to him. A frown on his face. Dropped eyebrows, opened lips. Confusion climbing over his anger.

The gentleman struggled back up. Bark clinging to his hands, mud on his shirt and neck. 'That is the truth of it, my good man.' He reached into his jacket and retrieved a slip of paper, which he handed to Ned's father. 'This is for your son, but if you need material proof of our trade, look no further.'

Ned's father took the cheque. Looked at it.

Ned saw his chance. 'It's not for me, Dad.' He tried to harden his voice. 'I know we need it.'

But he saw that his father wasn't listening. He saw how the violence had run from him, how the life in him had slackened. Saw how his mouth was still open, and his lips were moving, but nothing was coming out. His father rubbed at his face, rubbed hard, hard enough to be painful. Then he came towards Ned, slow, dazed. Pushed the cheque into his son's hand and took a few more steps before stopping where the dirt ended, where the rocks and sand began.

Ned heard his voice rise. 'It's twenty times what I paid for it. Closer to twenty-five! It has to help.'

In reply he received only the sound of his father's slow breaths.

Needles in Ned's eyes, needles in his throat. 'It has to!' The cheque screwing in his palm.

A scraping sound behind him. The gentleman was reapplying himself to the business of loading the boat. 'Of course it will, my boy. Money always does.' He braced his knees and gave a huge shove, managing to raise the rear half of the boat onto the trailer. It teetered. Deep scratches had been scored into the shellac. The gentleman clapped his hands, then went to his truck and retrieved a few lengths of rope.

More noise from the bush. Heavy thumps, and then Maggie and the mare crashed onto the beach. She slung herself to the ground before the mare had come to a stop. Ned's rifle was in her hands, its stock rising to her shoulder, its barrel pointed at the gentleman. 'Step away from my brother's boat.'

The gentleman took her in. Laughed, long and ugly. Laughed at Ned. 'Given your demeanour, my boy, I would never have imagined your family to be so dramatic.' He waved a hand at Maggie. 'Talk to your father. And rejoice! Your fortunes have changed, my dear.' He began throwing ropes over the boat, lurching around the trailer to tie them off.

Maggie lowered the gun. Saw their father, unmoving on the sand. Saw Ned coming to her side, showing her the cheque. She glanced at it.

'Oh, Ned.' Her face took on the same slackened look as their father's.

'It's not for me!' He flung an arm at the paddocks, at the orchard, at the hills. Could feel himself becoming angry. Wasn't it all obvious? Wasn't it necessary?

She released a shuddering sigh. There was so much sorrow in her: on her face, in her voice, in the soft slumping of her torso. 'It's not enough, Ned.'

'It'll help!' He knew he was shouting. Couldn't help it, didn't care. Couldn't understand their reactions. Had he not done the right thing? Had he not put what mattered most first? Who wouldn't want a brother who helped? Who wouldn't want a son who made sacrifices?

All he could see was his sister's sadness: a weary, lonely sadness. And beyond her, their father, still trying to breathe. His eyes on the river, the rest of him gone. Vanished but for his breath.

The bump of a door behind them. The gentleman had the boat loosely secured, and was leaning into the cabin of his truck. He emerged with a half-empty bottle of whisky. Four grimy glasses. He approached the Wests, winkling out the cork. Wet leaves patterning his suit. Saying something about a toast.

# 19

YEARS LATER. AN aeon after his boat had sailed off on the gentleman's trailer. After he'd toughed out all the things expected of him, yet still had more to do. After he'd shouldered his way into middle age, after he'd stacked up a little wealth, a little pain. After all that, Ned travelled south to Hobart, where Sally and Grace were studying at the university.

Driving down the Midlands for the first time in years showed him how much it had changed. He'd seen the development of his valley in real time, as mines had closed, towns had sprawled and a great white bridge had been built over the river. As almost all the orchards had been ripped out and replaced by vineyards. But he hadn't known how far forward the rest of the island had marched. Twice as many paddocks bordered the highway as he remembered. Twice as many fences, twice as many sheep. The road was wider, blacker, smoother. Vegetation and variation had been stripped away, and there was a new uniformity to the landscape: dry paddocks, bare trees and a bristling army of gorse, everywhere he looked. Gazing out his window to the east, he noticed the absence of certain forests that had once crawled over the low mountains. Caught himself missing them, hoping they would return. Recognised the hypocrisy in his wanting: the trees in those vanished forests had been manna gums. White Knights, felled on his watch.

That evening he met his eldest girls at a restaurant by the tightly packed waterfront. They ordered drinks, food. It was July. Black frost covered the cobblestones and an Antarctic wind was tearing through the streets. Ned shifted in his jacket, flexed his toes. He noticed how tired Sally and Grace were. Thought they might be hungover, or were studying too hard, but once they'd downed half their glasses the reason for their exhaustion came out: they'd spent the day walking in the mountains, and the trip hadn't gone as they'd planned. In the city the weather had been overcast but mild, and they'd driven west without concern. A ranger at the station near the start of the national park had told them there was a 'light dusting' of snow at the summit. They'd thanked her and kept driving, marvelling at the icy slabs by the side of the road. Oohing at the dark mist on the peaks, thinking nothing of what it might mean. Northern daughters to their core.

At the start of the walk they'd skirted a lake easily enough. Cracked thin films of ice over shallow puddles with their boots. The track then led them upwards to a rocky plateau, which they were to cross before descending through a weak forest of snow gums, back to their car.

When they reached the plateau it was covered in blanking whiteness. They saw the first trail marker in the distance, pushed through the snow towards it. Saw the glint of the next one. Kept thrashing their knees forward, fuelled by Sally's obstinacy, her implacable drive. Grace quiet in her wake. At the third marker the snow was at thigh height. They couldn't step on it without crashing down, rolling their ankles. They turned around, but could no longer see the markers behind them. Snow was falling again, gentle and thick, filling their tracks. They conferred, argued, despaired. Pushed on.

What should have been a two-hour walk lasted most of the day, as they churned through the snow, swaddled in mist, aiming for a forest they could not see. They ran out of food. Their noses stung. Their legs began to prickle. It was only when they stumbled into an invisible stream, trickling beneath the snow, that they were saved. Following its course meant plunging their boots into icy water with each step, water that found its way through their boots into the fibres of their socks, but it also meant they would inevitably find trees.

After an hour of sodden stomping they saw ghostly figures beckoning them through the dense cloud. Highland snow gums, colour-swirled and hardy, and alpine yellow gums, splashed with shades of lemon and olive. Skeletal in the mist. When they reached them, they saw fluorescent pink tags hanging from the twisting artwork of their branches. Orange bike lights hammered into dolerite boulders, beneath flakes of minty lichen. They dragged themselves along this trail, exhausted and numb, back to their car, where they cranked the heater, chipped off their frozen socks and drove back to the city to meet their quiet, fumble-mouthed father.

Beer fell down their throats. They stretched their calves.

Ned was thinking of their uncle Bill, and the time he'd climbed his own mountain, flailed through his own snow. He was about to tell his daughters the story, then realised that he still didn't know which version was true. Had Bill outmuscled and rescued a raging ram, or had he failed to save a wounded, weakened one? Ned had never found out. He couldn't start the tale without knowing the ending. He closed his mouth. Felt the raw throb he always did whenever he thought of Bill.

He also felt an angered itch. He wanted to tell his daughters how foolish they'd been. How close they'd come to a blackened foot, a sawn-off nose. Didn't they know what a bit of time in the snow could do to flesh? He thought he'd raised smarter girls, he wanted to say. But he couldn't say any of it, because he hadn't come to this freezing concrete port to tell them off. He needed to tell them about their mother.

But now they were warmed through, now the beer had got to work, and they wanted to talk about their lives on campus, their studies. The things they'd learned that had tilted and swollen their understanding of the world. Things their sheltered rural father needed to hear. Sally talking, Grace nodding.

The golden mean. Bundle pricing. The Charge of the Light Brigade. Supply and demand. The Bay of Pigs. The sunk-cost fallacy. Did he know about these things? Had these concepts and moments reached him on the orchard, in the forests, on the sheep stations, in the stockyards?

In this torrent of talk he could only smile, raise his eyebrows and say, oh, is that so; well, I'll be; this is all new to me. He wasn't offended, despite their youthful arrogance—he was too pleased to see how much his daughters were enjoying their learning.

The only problem in all this history, ethics and economics was that it left no room to speak about Callie. There was no opportunity for him to tell them that the cancer was back: maybe stronger than before, maybe not—it was too early to tell.

He tried to slow the conversation's pace, to steer the topic towards their mother. But Sally had leaned forward, put down her beer.

'Do you know about the orchard, Dad?'

He paused for a moment, confused. 'I know what there is to know. What do you mean?'

'I dunno.' A fierce light had come into Sally's eyes. 'About the people who were there first. You know, before the invasion.'

Ned stared at her. Couldn't understand what she was saying, what was happening. 'What's gotten into you?'

He noticed that Grace was looking away from them both, studying the lamplights through the windows.

Sally raised her hands. 'The invasion, Dad. I thought you'd at least know that your great-grandparents weren't exactly invited here.'

'Of course I bloody know...'

'About the killings?'

'Look, love, there are some things you don't understand...'

'Like massacres?'

'Don't you talk to me like that. Don't you dare.'

The words had come out harsh, loud. Sally flinched, retreated into her seat. Grace's shoulders fell, but she kept looking out the window.

Ned felt an instant burn of shame. 'Sorry, Sal. Sorry. It's just...Yes, I know a thing or two about that stuff. I've listened to the old folks around the valley. But I'm not here to talk about that. You see…'

And he tried to get it out. To tell them about Callie's sickness, how the cancer had reappeared in her breast and also in her blood. How a mastectomy was scheduled. Their mother was going to get through it, he needed to tell them, just as she'd got through it when they were children. They could be sure of it. Was there anyone stronger than their mother? Did they know any other mother who'd work in the trees all day and in the home all night? Any other woman who could hunt hawks in the morning and cut roses in the afternoon? If anyone was going to beat this thing, he needed to say, it would be Callie West.

That was all of it. He had it down, even the tone—a sombre heft to the serious news at the start and a dash of light-hearted optimism for the details at the end. But as he prepared himself to say it, other thoughts crept in. How lately Callie had lost her appetite and was existing mostly on tea. How even ten minutes in the garden—that garden she'd summoned and caressed out of the soil into existence—now exhausted her. How only the day before, as she slept in the valley's low afternoon light, he'd felt for her knee through the blanket and found a thin spike of bone. How slowly the doctor had spoken when he'd told them the diagnosis. How, before Ned left that morning, Callie had gripped his fingers, found her old boldness. 'Don't you lie to them, Ned. You give them the truth.'

He felt a sudden sharpness in his eyes, and blinked himself back into the present. Realised that he'd trailed off. He reached for words, but Sally filled the silence first.

'If you know so much,' she asked, 'then what's the river's name? Its real name.'

Ned stopped himself from snapping at her again. Tried to think. He'd heard it somewhere, once. He was sure. But it felt like his mind was wading against a current, and the name would not come to him.

'It's kanamaluka, Dad. It's called kanamaluka.'

'Ah, yes. That's right,' he said. 'Now listen, there's something your mother and I—'

'Did you ever think about giving it back?' The challenge was gone from Sally's voice. Now she was speaking softly, almost conspiratorially.

Ned stared at her.

'It's what some other people are doing,' she continued. 'Giving their land back. Or at least sharing it.' She reached over, put a hand on his wrist. 'Did you and Mum ever consider it?' She was speaking with a reasonable tone, as if it made all the sense in the world.

Ned felt the warmth of her palm. Wanted her to let go. 'I didn't drive all this way to talk about that. Listen, you girls need to—'

'Sal.' It was Grace, finally turning from the window to cut her father off. A new kind of weariness in her expression.

Sally blew out a breath. 'I'm just asking...'

'You can't expect all this of him. How's he meant to understand?' Grace turned to Ned. Gave him an apologetic smile. 'Sorry, Dad.'

Ned met her gaze. Felt her condescension tear a new wound in him. He felt off-balance, disoriented, angry. His daughters had never spoken to him like this before. Nobody had.

Sally sighed, picked up her drink.

He took a deep breath, shook off Grace's smile, shook Callie from his head and tried to focus on the question. A response began forming in him. Be serious, he wanted to say to them. You don't just give away an orchard. It's not what people do. Where would we have gone? Do you know how hard your mother and I worked for that place? Do you understand the blood and sweat we put into it? Did you not enjoy your childhood on that property, in that valley, on the banks of that river—of kanamaluka? Do you understand how lucky you've been?

He was annoyed—by his daughters' impertinence, by the question's implication, and by how it had distracted him from what he was there to do. If he didn't tell them about Callie now, with a bit of beer in him, he might never be able to get it out. Yet he also felt uneasy. Grace and Sally didn't know what they were talking about, he told himself. They were young, still children in many ways. But there it was: the nag of unease. The sting of truth.

He thought of how he'd prided himself on learning about the Letteremairrener people, and the Panninher who'd also lived in the valley, and the other tribes all over the island. He knew what had happened to them; he'd read Robinson's diaries when they were published; he was aware of what had been done. But he'd treated it all as history. In the course of his own life, he had done nothing about it.

So instead of bristling, instead of shouting, he just took a drink, faced Sally and said: 'No—no, we never thought about anything like that.'

They were quiet after that, all three of them. But the conversation had sent a rattle through Ned, and he felt the need to justify himself. I was there long before you were born, he wanted to say. I've known this kanamaluka longer than I've known your mother. And as he cast around for what that meant, how important his connection to the river was, his mind snagged on the little boat he'd once owned. How he'd freed it from a prison of thick lead paint. He wanted to tell his daughters about the glory he'd restored it to. How intoxicating the sight of it had been. How the scent of its timber had put him under a spell he had never truly recovered from. What discovering Huon pine does to a person. How it had rode the river so cleanly, so joyously, like a wish come true. How short his time with it was, how hard the summer had been, how he'd sold the boat to a rich little man, a stranger whose name he soon forgot. How it never carried him to the river mouth. I didn't get to go back, he wanted to tell his daughters. I didn't get to return to the place my father took us, your uncles and me, where the mad whale—do you remember the mad whale, do you remember the stories, did anyone ever tell you?—raised its twelve-foot tail above our borrowed boat, hiding the moon's light, poised to smash us into red flotsam. Only it didn't, he wanted to say. It could've, but it didn't. With colossal gentleness it lowered its flukes into the water beside us. Loosed a spray of vapour from its blowhole. Rolled onto its back and exposed to us the creamy striations of its belly. Twisted through the water so that the hugeness of its eye was close to us, a couple of yards from the boat. An eye shockingly familiar in its mammalian warmth. An eye filled with starlight: an eye lit by a half-dark heaven.

199

# 20

THE MORNING AFTER the sale of the boat found Ned on the porch, rinsed with gloom. He would no longer sail the river, tracing its contours, learning its truths. No longer would he know weightless adventure as he skipped across the water. Perhaps never again. He'd likely never see the boat again, either. If he wanted to explain its uncommon beauty and the effect it had on people, including himself, especially himself, he would have to use the blunt tool of description—could not show it to anyone, and allow it to speak for itself. He didn't even have a photograph.

There would now be no moment where his brothers would stand on the shore and watch him glide on the currents. They would never wait for him to swing the sail and come towards them. The boat and its captain—this masterly Ned of the river—would only ever exist as a debatable, possibly exaggerated anecdote. As far as his brothers would ever know—when Toby came back, if Bill came back—their warless little brother had spent a pleasant few months killing rabbits, buying a boat, repairing and then selling it before he went back to school. To them, that would be the extent of his work. That would be the story.

These thoughts made him remember something that had happened between the three of them not long before Bill enlisted. Perhaps only a week or two. Bill and Toby had been invited to a party a few orchards over, an end-of-year affair organised by a girl they went to school with. Ned wasn't on the list, was too young to even be thought of. But at ten o'clock his brothers hadn't come home, and his father told him to go fetch them.

They could hear the party, had been hearing it for hours. Noises flying across the paddocks, through the windows. Revelry mixed with crashes that had become louder and more frequent as the night ran on. At a particularly harsh one—the loud ring of something smashing into tin or iron—the old man stood up and gave Ned the order. His voice and movement sudden, almost violent. Ned didn't want to go; his brothers would be furious with him for interrupting the party. But their father was now staring out the window, wincing at each sound, so he did not talk back. He got a torch and put on his boots.

Outside the ground was wet, the air heavy. His torch-light tripped over the trees, which were taller and more severe in the darkness than under the sun. He followed the noises across Limberlost, over another orchard, up a driveway, until he reached their source: a packing shed. Coloured lights were blinking through its apertures. Yelling and singing poured from its door, as well as a kind of music Ned thought he hadn't heard before, until he realised it was just regular instruments played with too much rigour and not enough skill. Unsteady figures were coming in and out of the shed, arms linked, arms over shoulders, cigarettes burning into fingers and lips. Another group was the source of the crashing sounds: a few men throwing empty bottles onto the roof of the shed.

Ned hung back in the driveway. Turned off his torch. All these people were older than him. All looked drunk. None would be pleased to see him, least of all his brothers. He was trying to think of what to do, trying to gather enough courage to go inside, when the decision was taken away from him by two people coming out.

Bill was walking backwards, his hands clawed under Toby's armpits, dragging him into the night. Colour shone from Toby's face; something was smeared across his chin, his neck, his shirt. He was struggling in Bill's grip, kicking at the dirt. Still Bill pulled him away from the shed. Ned watched, not moving, not understanding, not knowing if he should go help, or which of his brothers he'd be helping. He ran forward a few steps, then stopped. Other people were coming out of the shed now. Some watching his brothers, some shouting at them.

Bill was twisting his neck, casting about for something. He saw Ned. Confusion filled his eyes, before his face whipped into sternness.

'Here.' His voice a sharp bark. 'Now.'

Ned ran over. Avoided looking at the growing crowd of people, looked only at his brothers. Bill's body was tensed as Toby thrashed against his strength. Toby swearing, Toby spitting. Ned could see now that blood ran from his nose and cream clotted his clothes. Golden pastry flecked his hair and cheeks.

Bill barked again. 'Get his feet.'

Ned obeyed. Toby noticed him, tried to kick him. Ned grabbed Toby's boots and held on tight, a squirming foot pressed against each side of his torso. Toby cursed them both, cursed the crowd over Ned's shoulder. Bill kept marching backwards, faster now that Ned was helping. He took them to a row of cars parked up against a water tank. With one hand he tested the boot latch of the first, and when they heard a pleasing click he flung it open.

'Lift him, Ned.'

Again Ned did as he was told. Bill tipped the upper part of Toby's body into the boot and Ned dropped the legs in. Bill slammed the lid shut. Muffled roars bounced through the metal. The car began to rock and thump. Bill climbed on top of the boot, pulled a lighter from his pocket, a cigarette from another, flared it to orange life. Ned hauled himself up beside Bill. Rode the thumps of Toby's knees and fists.

He waited. Let Toby wear himself out. Let the tension steam off Bill's skin. He felt the energy gathered within his eldest brother lessening with each long draw, each cloud of pushed smoke. When Bill began to breathe between puffs, Ned asked him what had happened.

Bill pulled again on the cigarette. 'Misunderstanding.' He rubbed his eyes. 'Between Tobe and Beatrice McKeown. Or her brother Greg. Or Mrs McKeown. Not sure. The three of them convinced him to take a dive through the platter table.'

Beneath them, Toby had quietened. Bill tilted his neck back and gave his smoke to the stars. Ned shifted his weight, put his hands in and out of his pockets. More people had spilled out of the party. He could hear crunching gravel and muttered anger, getting closer. He looked over and saw a group of young men coming towards them. Bottles in hands, lurches in their strides. The first one stopped before Bill. Ned couldn't see him well in the darkness, but from the hulk of his shoulders he could tell it was Greg McKeown. The McKeowns bred merinos, and the shearing and tossing of wool had shaped Greg into a rectangular lump. Ned had never spoken to him. Knew him only from the bus, from school, from watching him mash opposition football players into frosted grass as Toby paraded the oval's flanks.

He crossed his arms, planted his feet. 'Where's your brother?'

Bill kept staring upwards. Kept blowing smoke. 'Having a lie down.'

'Where?'

Now Bill looked down, straightened his gaze. Let his eyes harden on the face in front of him. 'Mars.'

Ned felt his pulse fly. Greg held Bill's stare. He snorted. Rolled his shoulders. Swore at him, swore at Ned, then turned and stalked off, swigging from his bottle. His companions followed. Ned felt adrenaline leak out of him. After they were back inside the shed he looked around at the vehicle they were sitting on.

'Whose car is this?'

Bill sucked on his cigarette. Took it from his mouth, held the smoke deep.

Ned heard the broken music start back up. 'Dad says it's time to come home.'

'Dad's probably right.' But Bill didn't get off the trunk. He kept pulling a glow into the cigarette. Kept blowing long, slow clouds of smoke into the ink-dark sky.

As Ned remembered that night from his position on the porch, boatless and miserable and more alone than he'd felt all summer, he was jarred by a realisation: that party had been a fortnight before Bill's eighteenth birthday. He had known he was about to enlist. As they sat together on the boot that was caging their brother, not speaking, smoke filling the night between them, Bill had been aware of what lay before him. Had known he wasn't far from gone.

~

Later that morning Jackbird and Callie came to Limberlost. It was odd for them to appear together; all summer Ned had watched as Jackbird tried to cultivate the persona of a dashing outsider, a role which did not have room for a younger sister, while Callie had gripped her shotgun, patrolled her paddocks, and come to decide that her older brother was both deluded and an idiot.

Ned was glad to see them. All morning his father and sister had hovered about him like injured moths. The old man had given him no chores. Maggie had lent him a book, which was in his hands as Jackbird and Callie approached. He was looking at its pages, taking none of the words in. It had been their mother's favourite since childhood, Maggie had told him. *A Girl of the Limberlost*. The book from which their mother had taken the name for the orchard, seeing in their valley the same colours and dreams of the forest she'd read about in the novel.

Ned wanted to read it. Wanted to find in its pages the images and sensations that his mother had. Wanted something to root him to the earth, now that the river was out of his reach. But he couldn't focus, couldn't blunt the spikes in his thoughts, so he was happy to see Jackbird and Callie, glad that the sight of them together gave him something else to be curious about. He put his mother's book down and began walking towards them. Met them in the driveway.

Jackbird forced a grin. 'Morning, Neddy.'

Ned studied them. Saw the awkwardness and hesitancy in Jackbird. Saw how Callie, her arm no longer slung but still held against her body, was looking at the ground. Her usually fearless eyes avoided his.

Apprehension jostled his curiosity. 'What's all this, then?'

Jackbird scratched his neck. 'Your boat...'

'I sold it.'

'Oh. That makes sense.' Jackbird twisting on his heels, twisting at his hip. Something kinking him up. 'Because, well...'

For the first time that Ned could remember, his friend struggled to speak. Ned's dread swelled. The silence was bitter and awful. Eventually, after a few false starts, Jackbird managed it. Got it all out in a tripping torrent. When he was finished, Callie looked up. Tried to tell Ned how sorry she was, but she was talking to air, to rising dust. He was already gone.

~

He'd left his bike by the boatshed, so he took the mare. Had no time to feel the usual trepidation as he approached her, threw on her saddle, threw himself onto her back. Kicked her up the driveway. For a moment he worried that she wasn't yet up to galloping, but she ran strong, pulling at the bit. He leaned into her neck.

Sweat cooled his face, stung his eyes. Up the driveway they went, through the gate. Onto the road, turning right, heading towards the highway. The sped-up valley clung at his peripheries. They raced up a hill and around the first, second, third bends. On the fourth he saw the first signs of what Jackbird had told him—grooves cut into the gravel. Around the next corner these markings deepened and took off at crazed angles, snaking over themselves.

One corner remained before the road straightened. A corner everyone in the area knew well. A sudden corner that sneaked up in daylight and reared up alarmingly in darkness. He and the mare crashed towards it, following the swerving pattern in the gravel until it ended at a steep bank.

A copse of gums towered over the road. Ancient, burl-trunked hardwoods. The kind whose siblings and cousins had defanged colonial saws, blunting and ruining their iron teeth. Timber that was harder than many kinds of rock. Hard enough to crumple the bodies of speeding trucks while bearing no greater wounds than a few patches of torn bark, a few teardrops of gluggy sap.

A truck hadn't hit these eucalypts, but its cargo had. From the shape of the churned gravel it seemed the driver had been going too fast, his trailer jack-knifing behind his vehicle. At this final bend it had swung wildly towards the bank, and as the driver had righted the truck the trailer had been yanked roadward, right at the corner's elbow. This violent correction had caused it to throw its load. Frayed ropes, lying in the dirt, confirmed this theory. So did the presence of the load itself, lying at the base of the unyielding eucalypts in splintered, glowing pieces.

Ned stared at the dry wreckage of his boat. Not his, he numbly thought, feeling for the wrinkled cheque still shoved in the back pocket of his shorts. And though his sense of ownership lingered, what lay before him could no longer truthfully be called a boat. Its meeting with the gums had split it into a number of distinct parts. The bow had broken near the centreboard and been torn from the planks of the boat's middle and stern. It lay beside the road, bristling with fibrous, delicate splinters at each point of violent separation. The back section of the boat hung in the air, impaled on a large limb that had punched a ragged hole into the hull. The mast had snapped off into the scrub: a polished rod in a gang of crooked limbs. The oars were strewn in the dirt. The oak rudder, hurled by the collision, lay on the other side of the road.

The mare clopped over to the carnage. Sniffed at the green-gold fragments scattered across the gravel. Shook her head at the richness of the scent, richer than Ned had ever smelled before. The rending of the timber had released a huge, dense cloud of Huon pine fragrance into the air. It filled the world with heady spice, and Ned could not escape it, could not blow it from his nostrils, could breathe and taste nothing else but the perfume of his boat's death.

# 21

MANY YEARS LATER, Callie suggested Ned go talk to a doctor. It made no sense to him. She was the one who needed a doctor. Her current ones, including all the specialists, were saying the same thing: that her latest illness would be her final one. They didn't all agree that her cancers had been caused by the orchard sprays—it was impossible to know, they said, which only made Ned surer that it was true—but they agreed that there was nothing else they could do. Months. Maybe weeks. Yet there Callie was, sitting calmly in her chair, telling Ned he needed medical help.

They'd left their little orchard a few years earlier. Had sold up, moved closer to Launceston, to a brick house on a hill overlooking the part of kanamaluka where the water turned from fresh to salt. It was a pleasant spot. Ned had a few apple trees, a few plums and apricots. He had an unbroken view of the water that had flowed alongside him his whole life. But Callie was not getting better.

Their daughters had all come and were helping: cooking, cleaning, fretting. Ned and Callie's grandchildren—four of them now, all under five—were at their own homes, with their fathers. There was nothing for Ned to do other than to make tea, go to the pharmacy, see to his meagre trees. He ignored Callie's suggestion at first, thought she was being ridiculous. But she must have mentioned it to Sally or Grace, definitely Harriet, because then all three were urging him to book an appointment. You need to, they said. We can tell how stressed you are. It'll help. You need to talk to someone. It'll help.

He only did it so they'd stop hassling him. So they'd return their attention to their mother. The doctor was an older man, about his own age. He asked Ned to sit down and explain what the matter was. Ned tried to tell him there was no problem, other than the fact his wife was dying, that was the problem; he personally had no problems, was hale and hearty, and was only here because his family had forced him.

The doctor nodded. Put down his notepad, did not dispute anything Ned had said. Just leaned back in his chair, and asked Ned about what life had been like before his wife was dying. Ned stared at the doctor. Didn't know what was happening. Clammed up. It's all right, the doctor told him. You're clearly in fine health. But you've paid for this appointment, so we may as well have a chat.

Ned, seeing the logic, relented. Began answering the questions: what he enjoyed, what made him happy, what made him relaxed. He wasn't used to talking like this, but he gave it a shot. What made him angry, what made him upset. The doctor nodded along, taking no notes. Then, with gentleness, in an offhand tone, he asked Ned to ponder why these things made him happy and relaxed and angry and upset. Why he was the way he was.

Ned baulked. I don't know, he said. No bloody idea. Who knows these things? I grow apples. I look after my family. I don't hate a beer or two. I'm like everyone else where I'm from.

Then tell me about that, said the doctor. What it's like where you're from.

Ned said he didn't see the point. Try anyway, asked the doctor. What harm can it do?

So he did. He tried. He spoke about the valley. About Limberlost. Didn't mention his parents or siblings, didn't want to be analysed like that. Mostly he talked about Callie, because that's why he was there. About the long love of their marriage.

That's what it was, he said to the doctor. I mean, that's what it is, a love that has endured and strengthened—I don't need to explain it, do I? Without her, Ned felt like he wasn't fully there. Like he'd been watered down. Light milk.

She knows everything about me, he said. Always has. He'd never been able to keep a secret from her. Not in the marriage, not since they were children. They'd known each other that long, he told the quiet doctor. He could never hide a thing from her, not even the quoll he once accidentally trapped. Striking little fellow. She helped him care for it, release it. Maybe that was the start of it, he told the doctor. Hard to know. But he'd always appreciated it. Just as he'd appreciated how she'd come to tell him what had happened to his boat. Had come to say it to his face.

'Boat?' The doctor had leaned forward. But Ned was no

longer looking at him. His eyes were on the floor, and he was talking about the moment he'd rode up to the boat's remains. He realised he hadn't told the doctor anything else about the boat, hadn't given his story context, but he couldn't stop. It was all flinging out of him. How long he'd stared at the wreckage. How he'd tried to tell himself that it didn't matter, that he'd sold it. That there was no reason for him to mourn something that wasn't his.

And yet, he said, he still fell to his haunches, his breathing all wrong, tears muddying the dust on his face, his hands scrabbling at chunks of shattered Huon pine. He'd begun gathering the scattered parts, seeing where they'd been shorn off, trying to align them like a jigsaw puzzle. Like a puzzle from his nightmares. How, as he pushed a golden fragment into a messy wound on the hull, he'd fallen over. Couldn't get his breaths in. What's that called? he asked the doctor. Hyperventilating? Or just choking? How he'd lain on his back, stared up at the iron-hard gums and sucked at the air until his throat seized still.

# 22

WHEN OXYGEN EVENTUALLY found its way into his lungs, Ned got to his feet, turned from the crash site and rode back to Limberlost. He felt as if a thread that ran up his spine and into his brain had been snipped clean near the base of his skull. He imagined that this was what being drugged felt like. Or being shot, or losing a limb. Occasionally he would howl at the hard-woods, bellow at the gravel. Other times he'd laugh, loud and delirious.

He considered riding past the driveway, down to the river. He thought about leaping from the mare and striding into the water, striding and then stroking and then diving to that place of clean nothingness: the cold floor of sand. A dark, shifting ceiling above him. Staying there, not coming out. But when they reached the entrance to Limberlost the mare turned into the driveway, and he let it take him home.

In the kitchen he found Maggie, told her what had happened.

Her reaction was instant: her eyes wide, her voice urgent. 'Have you deposited the cheque?'

Ned felt his lungs tighten all over again. He threw down his sandwich and tore into Beaconsfield on the mare, tethered her outside the bank and rushed inside. The clerk at the counter told him that the cheque would take a few days to clear. Maybe a week. Ned began to sweat, to shake. He begged her to do something faster, begged her to call someone, to confirm the account.

The teller hesitated. 'I suppose I could call the head branch. Have them check. But it's not standard practice, you see.'

'Please.' Ned was hanging on the counter. Holding himself up.

She hesitated again. Looked at her colleagues. Eventually gave him a swift nod, then strode to a telephone at the rear of the room, cheque in hand.

As he waited, Ned began to see the gentleman as he truly was: a sly conman. A thief. And he realised that for this to be true, Ned had played the role of victim—an unsavvy rural fool. He rocked on his heels, and began to count the violence he'd committed against the valley's rabbits all summer. Catalogued the wounds, measured the blood. Imagined re-enacting all of it upon the gentleman's whisky-rinsed body.

The teller returned, smiling. She'd spoken to the manager of the branch where the cheque had been drawn. There were sufficient means to ensure that the cheque would be cleared. It was certain.

Ned felt like he might fall down again, like he had on the road. He thanked the teller, asked her to deposit the money into his father's account and stumbled out into the sunlight.

When Ned told Maggie that the money had gone through, she softened. Began treating him the way she had at breakfast: gentle, stilted, ashamed. She made tea, told him how sorry she was about the boat. Told him she admired what he'd done. That while the money wasn't enough, he had been right: it would help, somewhat. He shouldn't have done it, she said. He had earned that boat. She and their father had been so impressed, so proud. He should at least have talked it over with her. But the money would help.

For the next week she trod lightly around him, as if he was recovering from an illness. Asking him he how he was, offering to make him food. He didn't want food, he nearly shouted. The bread was hard and the potatoes soft. He wanted something to do, something to love. He had no rabbits to hunt, no quoll to hide and heal, no boat to revive and sail. Nowhere to push his imagination, nothing to dream of, nothing but the golden planks of savaged timber that floated into his mind whenever he was able to sleep. Nowhere to turn his thoughts from reality. No hiding from the orchard's problems. No distraction from the letter that would eventually come from the army, the one they knew was inevitable. It's been months, he wanted to shout at Maggie. He was cut loose from the anchors he'd been dropping all summer. He'd never felt so brotherless.

~

Worse than his sister was his father. He would hang in doorways, staring at Ned as if trying to think of something to say. Nothing ever came to his lips. Before the boat, his father used to forget Ned was around, would fail to hear Ned when he spoke. Now Ned kept finding the old man staring at him like he would an injured dog, a blighted tree. Like the corpse of a stranger who'd once asked him for shelter.

Ned hated it. Didn't want this kind of attention—wanted only for him to wake up as the man Ned had known as a child: a man who winked and laughed and let everything slide off him, like he'd been oiled against life's rigours. A man who could rip the hide off a rabbit, no blade in his hand.

Ned felt that he'd waited long enough, that he'd done enough. Had done everything he could in the absence of his brothers. Couldn't his father keep his side of this bargain, the one Ned had never told him about? Couldn't he reform himself into the man he'd been a decade earlier? A man of action. A man with answers. A man unafraid of monsters. The only man able to see through the beery gossip of the valley—who, in response to the hysteria, had taken his terrified sons to the river mouth. Had motored them towards death, had plunged them into its lair. Had met the wind's chill with a grin and a whistle. Had not moved, not an inch, as a whale exploded from the water a few yards from their boat.

That was the man Ned wanted back. The man who'd locked eyes with a giant in the night, then turned to his shivering sons and said, 'They're resting.'

A long silence followed, until one of them spoke.

'They?' It was Bill. Standing up gingerly, coatless and cold, holding his arms against his chest.

Their father cast an arm towards the water behind the rolling whale. Toby and Ned stood up too, followed the line of their father's arm, and saw a second creature bobbing above the surface. A similar shape, but much smaller. Little peaks of smooth flesh, bumping against the first whale's bulk.

'It's her calf.' Their father's voice was warm in the darkness. 'They travel up the coast, up from Antarctica, all the way to Queensland, where they give birth. Then they turn around and come back. Long trip. Sometimes they get tired, and need somewhere to rest where their calves will be safe.'

'What about the shipwrecks?' It was Toby. Suspicion in his shaking voice.

'Lies, drink—and the reef.' Their father pointed out past the heads. 'Mostly the reef.'

They watched the whales float in the murk, blowing spray into the air. After a minute, the mother showed them her eye again, unblinking and huge. Then she and her calf dipped back under the surface. It was an impossible thing: so many tons of flesh, disappearing in an instant. Their tails emerged fifty yards away, saluting the stars. Hanging high and wide. Ned's father started the motor.

'She's as interested in us as we are in dragonflies.' The engine smoked to life. He let it idle. Turned to his sons. 'If you're going to fear something, boys, it's best to understand it.' He laid a hand on Ned's scalp, his rough skin stilling Ned's shivers. 'To come right up against it.'

# 23

WHEN THE SUMMER died, it went quietly. There was no final exclamation of heat, no furious storms, no flourish of violence. The season just came to an end, and lay down. Instead of constant stifling dryness the days began to hold whole catalogues of weather: dewy mornings, warm lunchtimes, gusty nights. Skirts of rain drifted over Limberlost on little skips of wind, greening the grass, brightening the leaves. The sky shifted from brittle blue to something softer, a pale colour interrupted by streaks of thin, uncertain clouds. At dusk, it glowed peach and salmon. Beneath it, the river lay steely and waveless, cut only by the eternal rhythm of its whirlpools. The sun retreated. Autumn's grace crept forward.

Ned had a week left on the orchard. At the end of it he'd be on a bus, heading south to Launceston, to a new school term. To cricket matches played on ovals covered in sheep shit. Later, in winter, he'd play football on those same ovals, and have his body brutalised and numbed across long patches of stubborn frost that lingered on the turf until noon. He'd have lessons, tests, exams. Trigonometry that came easily to him—the unvarnished honesty of numbers—and English composition that didn't. French that evaded him like a fistful of fog. There would be girls—not at his school, but girls in town, girls on the bus, girls at sister schools. Jackbird's elbow in his ribs, Jackbird's whistles in his ear. Ned's eyes bouncing off necks and ankles onto grey gutters.

It had been ten days since the sale and destruction of his boat. In that time he hadn't left the property. He'd helped his father in the trees and fetched eggs from the chicken coop. He'd scrubbed and peeled potatoes. Callie and Jackbird had each come by a few times, but he'd fobbed them off with lies about chores. Most afternoons he'd taken the mare out, sometimes riding, sometimes walking beside her. Moving over the orchard's hills and gullies, skirting its boundaries. Going nowhere near the water.

He tried to not think about the boat, but in many ways it was still there. In the flattened ferns near the shoreline. In the hollow boatshed visible from the farmhouse. In the memories that refused to stop rushing through him. Most days he woke up and looked out his window, checking the wind and weather, before he remembered that it was gone. He only had to close his eyes and lean into a breeze to find himself back on its bobbing deck. Only had to run a palm down the handle of an axe to remember the grains of the Huon pine. He wondered when these memories would relax: when he would be able to think of the boat not with awful grief, but with fondness. With a splash of the joy it had given him.

He tried to lose himself in physical activity. In parading through the apple trees, checking heavy fruit that had survived the storms. If there was no work on offer, he would find something to watch. The hopping dance of a juvenile magpie, its feathers mottled grey, its steps unsure. The searching pecks of chickens as they picked around the yard. The evening scuttle of brushtail possums as they muscled up and down gums. And at dawn the movement of rabbits, bouncing out of the undergrowth to graze on the revived grass. With the rain and coolness they'd come back. Returning from a dream he'd almost forgotten.

~

Ned was watching the rabbits one morning when the stillness was broken by the cough of an engine. He looked to the road and saw a truck paused at Limberlost's gate. A figure got out from the passenger side. Smoke blew from the truck's exhaust. It rolled off, and the figure began walking down the driveway.

Ned put down his mug of tea, his plate of toast. Lately he'd been eating breakfast outside. Sitting at the table with his sister and father, listening to their careful talk, fielding their gentle questions: it had all been too much work. It was easier to go out, to settle his thoughts by looking for twitching fur.

He watched the figure approach. It was a man. Thin, coming slow, with a slight limp.

Ned felt anger tighten him. Another gawker. Whoever he was, he clearly hadn't heard what had happened to the boat. Ned brushed crumbs from his hands and began moving towards the driveway. He knew he should be polite, but already he was struggling to stay calm. He wanted to shout at this stranger. To berate him for his rudeness, to chase him from the property. To tell him: It's gone! There's nothing for you here! I sold it, and it was torn into splinters! Go up the road, to the sharp bend. Sniff at its remains. Go have a whiff of what's left of it, if you must.

It was early too. Far too early to come visiting. Ned's anger gripped, burned. He stared at the man, noting his slim frame. He tensed the muscles in his neck. Felt sure he could handle this waifish stranger. Could throw him to the gravel and drag him off the property by his collar if he had to.

The man, now halfway down the driveway, had stopped. As if resting, or looking for something. Ned gathered the words in his throat. Knew that he was going to lose control. Tasted iron on his tongue. Got ready to shout.

Before he could, he heard a scrabbling at his back. He turned to see Maggie coming out of the house. Running along the driveway. Her feet skimming over the dirt, hair whipping out behind her. The memory of her turning the rifle onto the suited man flashed into him.

Ned became worried. Even though this man was uncommonly thin, even though he looked badly worn, he might be dangerous. He began to stride faster, trying to catch up, but he was too far behind her.

Maggie reached the stranger and, without slowing down, hurled her body into his. Ned flinched. Thought she had tackled him, before realising that they were embracing. Her arms wrapped around him. Her head was on his chest, her back heaving with what seemed to be sobs. The man stayed upright, braced against her weight, against the force of her.

By now Ned was trotting. Was close enough to see the man better. Close enough to see his face when he raised it.

Bill looked at him over their sister's shaking shoulder. His cheeks were sunken, his chin and brow more prominent than Ned remembered. Rough lines ran across his forehead and around his eyes: creases that could be wrinkles, could be scars. A newish shirt hung awkwardly on his spindly limbs and narrow trunk. His shoulders remained broad, but wore no flesh; they were all points and angles. His hair was thin too, and darker. His eyes had been pulled back into shadowed caves, and from those blackened divots he was staring at Ned. His eyes still a crisp blue. Still sharp.

A small smile drew his mouth open. His body slumped a little. Maggie clung on.

In that moment Ned felt a swelling, a ripping expansion, a hugeness that rang through him for the length of his life, a feeling that was sometimes rivalled but never quite matched. Not at weddings, not at births, not at funerals. Not when he worked his way north to Longreach, where he finally saw Toby again, finding him cocky, funny and largely unchanged. Not during good seasons or bad. Not when he was alone on cold waterways, not when he was in the grip of people he loved. Not as he poured dirt into graves, not as he watched his children, then his grandchildren, play. Not on the white sands of hidden beaches. Not in the shade of ancient trees, in whose canopies he imagined he could see the darting of cream-brown quolls. Not on rocky mountain roofs. Not in the presence of whales, not while viewing fine ships. Not at the scent of Huon pine. Not as Callie's last breath eased out of her, in their house overlooking kanamaluka, the eastern sun warming her face right up to the final moments of her life. Not at his ninetieth birthday, surrounded by his family and what was left of his friends, as he felt both powerfully loved and profoundly alone.

Not even then, at the very end of his life, did he feel it again, although he always remembered it: this hugeness of feeling. This undamming of a whole summer's fear, this half-sickening lurch to joy. This sight of his eldest brother coming home.

~

Ned was shaking. He could hear the banging of his blood. His knees were bending. He put a hand out to steady himself, found nothing to grasp. His lungs and throat hurt. Every inch of him was too hot.

A sound came from the porch. He swivelled to see his father looming in the doorway. The old man's cup hanging slackly in his hand, tea trickling from its lip to drench the doormat. His eyes wet, his mouth loose, his face a shining mess. His chest ballooning. Breaths rushing out of him, leaving him ragged.

Ned turned back to his brother, alive in the driveway. He felt Bill's eyes on him. Felt their hard, loving light.

## ACKNOWLEDGMENTS

Much of this book was written while I was the inaugural Hedberg Writer-in-Residence at the University of Tasmania. Thank you to the university, especially Robert Clarke and everyone in the School of Humanities, and to the Copyright Agency for funding the residency.

Thank you also to Bruce and Mary Hewitt, Emily Bill, Chris Arnott, David Winter, David's mum, Michael Heyward, James Roxburgh, Ric Crouch, everyone at Text Publishing and Atlantic Books, the Thomas Dewhurst Jennings Society, Red Jelly, The20, and everyone in my family, near and far.

## ALSO AVAILABLE FROM TEXT PUBLISHING

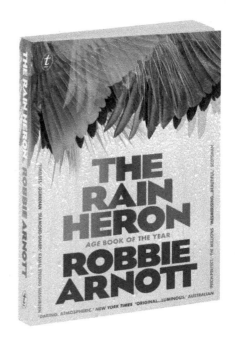